One Last Drop

One Last Drop
By Nicole Field

Published by Less Than Three Press LLC

All rights reserved. No part of this book may be used or reproduced in any manner without written permission of the publisher, except for the purpose of reviews.

Edited by V.E. Duncan
Cover designed by Aisha Akeju

This book is a work of fiction and all names, characters, places, and incidents are fictional or used fictitiously. Any resemblance to actual people, places, or events is coincidental.

First Edition August 2017
Copyright © 2017 by Nicole Field
Printed in the United States of America

Digital ISBN 9781684310562
Print ISBN 9781684310739

One Last Drop

NICOLE FIELD

Chapter One

Rory felt an attack of indecision as she stared at the people already gathered at the end of the hall. Unlike the meeting rooms, the kitchen and living room spaces were brightly lit, stark. She wouldn't be able to avoid anyone's gaze once she stepped in there. At the moment, she was still safe. Nobody had seen her. A part of her wanted to keep it that way: not moving forward, not moving back.

One foot forward. Then another. Chin high and heart pounding, Rory fixed her eyes on the fridge. If she didn't make eye contact… A part of her knew the idea was stupid. It wasn't like she could deny her presence here if she didn't look at anyone. Yet, just for now, it gave her the strength she needed to walk through this hallway and out to the other side. For just right now, she could ignore the room beyond the kitchen, the room where the Alcoholics Anonymous group met in the northern suburbs of Melbourne.

"Hello." It was the person standing beside the fridge who greeted her. Rory noted he had a nametag over his left breast pocket and hoped desperately that she wouldn't have to wear one herself. "First time?" He had a friendly face, and she could see that he was doing his best to put her at ease.

"Uh, yeah," Rory said shortly, looking towards him and away again. There was a check off list where people were meant to write their names and pay the couple of dollars that covered the room hire. Gratefully, Rory noticed the sheet also listed how much she needed to pay, so she didn't need to ask.

She found a handful of change in her pocket that added up to almost the amount she was supposed to pay.

"I'll pay in the rest I owe next week," she mumbled, still not looking at the man in front of her. God, he probably thought that she was some bum off the streets. She wasn't dressed particularly well or anything, but her jeans didn't have holes in them, and her blonde hair was brushed and tied back even if her face was devoid of makeup. It wasn't like she'd left her place intending to come here tonight. It just kind of... happened.

"That's okay." She could hear the smile in his voice and hazarded a look up. It didn't seem like he was judging her. The smile in his voice went all the way up to the twinkly eyes. The smile Rory summoned back for him wasn't her most sincere or convincing. It felt stiff on her face, but it was a smile, and it was the best she could do right now.

"In there?" she said through numb lips that told her that she needed to move before she lost her nerve entirely. Her hand pointed flaccidly towards the living room space.

"That's right," he answered before lifting his head to greet the next person to arrive.

Rory was glad she no longer held his attention. She found a seat near the window and looked down at the hard wood floor. A couple of other attendees were talking softly to each other. She imagined they knew each other from past meetings. From the shoes and pants she could see out of the corner of her eye, they didn't look as though they were straight off the streets, either. Maybe Rory had been guilty of projecting stereotypes herself. Maybe no one else here was thinking the same judgmental thoughts she was.

Many of the chairs in the hardwood floor living room weren't yet full. Rory concentrated on breathing in and out. It would be good if it was a small group, she told herself. Less confronting.

Eventually, the facilitator closed the door between kitchen and living room. His voice spoke up as everyone else quietened down.

"Okay, so we've got a few new people here tonight. For those of you who don't know me, my name is Jake, and I'm the facilitator of this meeting. This is a safe space where everyone can talk about the struggles they've been having. If you don't want to talk and just want to listen, that's fine, too. We try to avoid subjects like sex or politics or anything that might cause inflammatory language. Please remember that things that are shared in session are private and don't leave this room, and, of course, please turn off your phones. We'll be having a short tea break at around 8:30, and then we'll finish up at around 9:30."

He lapsed off into silence. Nobody else spoke. After several minutes of uncomfortable silence, Rory looked around her. Nobody else was speaking. Was she doing something wrong? Were people waiting for her to talk because it was her first time?

Just as she was about to crack—to speak—someone else in the group did so first. Rory heaved an internal sigh of relief before tuning in to pay attention to the other person's story. A balding man in middle age introduced himself as Mark. He talked about how he'd lost his wife and children, and that had been the wake-up call he'd needed to realise he had a problem.

Mark's story broke some unspoken code in the group. For the next hour until the mid-point break, stories flowed around each other, a combination of stories from new people, and some ongoing issues voiced by the regulars.

Still, it wasn't until after the break that she managed to work up a second bout of courage.

"Now we've just come back from break," said Jake. "I'd like to encourage anyone who came with something they wanted to talk about to speak up, especially if they haven't already."

Again, that silence. That wrathful, miserable

silence. But this time Rory didn't misunderstand it. It made her more willing to speak. "Um. My name is Rory. I go to the university not far from here. I'm, um… drinking most weekends. Some weeknights too. It's been worrying me."

Rory took a breath, worn out by that handful of short sentences. After a shuddering exhale, she started again.

"I'm worried because there have been two times in the last week that I've woken up, and there's been someone I don't know in the bed with me. I don't… remember what happened. Whether I've…" Rory ducked her head. She couldn't admit that in a room full of strangers. That she didn't know whether she'd been… raped.

She'd gotten an STI check immediately, the day after it happened. She cried when the test came back clear. The pregnancy test she'd bought from the chemist came back clear, but she also took the morning after pill in case he hadn't used a condom just to be sure, but it was too soon to know for sure on that yet.

Even as she ran through all of this, on top of what had actually been done to her, tears came to her eyes. She couldn't look at anyone in the room. "I… I'm worried I'm not strong enough. To keep… standing up to the temptation of the alcohol."

There. She'd said that much at least. But, instead of it being a weight off her mind, a load off her shoulders, Rory felt heavier than ever. She couldn't meet the eyes of anyone in the room; just a room full of strangers who shared a similar experience with her.

"I understand that."

Rory's gaze darted up at the sudden, unfamiliar voice. The face that looked back at her was that of a man not too much older than her, sitting next to the balding man who'd spoken earlier. This was the first time he'd said anything. His eyes met hers as he paused, making sure that she was done and he had permission to speak further.

"I remember being in uni, all that party culture. I remember reaching for the next beer mindlessly because it meant the conversation could go on for longer." The other man's gaze dropped, as though he'd been struck by the same malady that had stopped her from looking at the other attendees of the group.

Shame, Rory realised. That was what it was.

"For me," he continued, "I never felt more alive than when I had that beer, or cider, or spirit, in my hand. Classes, friends, family; all of that felt hollow, shadowy, unreal. I wasn't alive until the sun set, or I was in someone's dorm room, and it was time to drink."

Rory lip parted. Alive. Yes. That was how she felt. But…

"But is it ever worth it?" she asked. Asked him. Asked the group. "Is it worth that sinking feeling in the pit of your stomach when you wake up and realise your memories aren't all there? The regret?"

"No." This time it was the balding man speaking up again, shaking his head. "No. None of it's worth it."

Again, Rory was brought back to how much he'd lost. His kids. His family. Rory couldn't imagine losing herself so deep in partying that she could let that happen. But who was she to judge, really? She was here tonight, just like him.

Rory stopped in on the toilet on the way out, eagerly looking for the sign of red that would show a period that had begun, but to no avail. With a heavy sigh, she flushed the toilet, washed her hands and tried to pretend that everything was fine, as she'd done every day since the last party.

She felt a little sick, but better too. The sickness felt nothing like the sinking sensation she'd described during the session. She refused to consider it might be morning sickness.

It was the drop of adrenaline, she was pretty sure, even though she knew little about sports and even less about body physiology. High school health had been more like a benign sex ed, and she'd never had any interest in the Australian Football League. But she decided to put it down to a possible adrenaline drop because it was the most comforting thing to come to mind.

It was dark when she went outside. The crisp Melbourne air in autumn mingled with the slight dampness in the air. The oak trees that lined either side of this street in Coburg had littered red, orange, and yellow leaves in various stages of decomposition. Half a dozen had fallen on the windshield of her car just in the duration of the meeting.

Rory sat inside the car without turning the engine on and made a couple of promises to herself. She would not be having a celebratory drink the next time she finished an assignment for one of her classes. She would not be going to a party this weekend. She would stop drinking.

Only once she'd repeated these promises to herself a couple of times did she turn the key in the ignition and make her way back home.

Chapter Two

Rory sat with her hair haphazardly piled atop her head in a messy bun. She was at her favourite table at her favourite restaurant, Kismet. Unfortunately, the habit of sitting here was also very distracting. She was here often enough that she recognised all the staff. Back in her first years at uni, she'd volunteered a couple of shifts here before she filled her days with partying more often than not. Most of the people who had worked here at that time had since moved on. But there were still enough people who remembered her from back then that she had waitresses sitting at the table next to her on their way out for smoke breaks.

Kismet was located on a busy stretch of High Street in Northcote, a ten-minute drive from either her uni or the AA meeting community house, just far enough from both that she felt untethered by who she was in either of those places. Here she was just someone who liked the time out to type on her laptop or read a book and chat with people whose company she enjoyed on a very casual basis. Part of the allure of the wait staff here was that they never invited her to go out drinking with them, and she never felt obliged to go out with them.

The assignment she was currently working on only took up half her attention. The rest of her was keenly aware of how long it had been since her last drink. Four days. That, on its own, was okay. She'd gone twice as long without having a drink before, recently even. But the fact that she intended not to drink again had become its own difficulty. Every time she picked up a soft drink or coffee mug, she thought of what she *could* be drinking. She eyed the half empty cup of coffee in front of her with distaste, trying not to imagine the liquors that would mix well with it.

She only realised she was glaring furiously when she lifted her gaze slightly to meet the eyes of a stranger who had caught the expression and was now looking at her with amusement. Rory's frown morphed into apologetic embarrassment. Did the girl think she'd been glaring at her? Probably not. Not if Rory had read the amusement right. Maybe she just thought she was glaring at her assignment. She surely hadn't given off a vibe that would make a complete stranger think she was thinking of spiking her own coffee.

Rory couldn't make herself meet the other girl's gaze again.

For fifteen minutes, Rory found herself inordinately focused on her assignment. It was a good thing, and she avoided logging into the free wi-fi available and checking her social media. She realised that she knew what she wanted to write, and as soon as the focus came, so did the words. She smiled when she looked down at the word count and realised that she only needed another 200 words to hit the minimum word count and still had another point she wanted to make.

"Can I get you another drink?" One of the waitresses, a new girl, came back to her table, breaking Rory's attention. Out of the corner of her eye, Rory glanced to see if the other girl was still at her place two tables away. She was, her head dipped, deep in the novel she was reading.

"Another coffee?" Rory said absently. Then she realised that would be her third coffee since sitting here, and she changed her mind. "Uh, actually, just a hot chocolate." Plus, it was less common to put spirits into hot chocolate. Rory didn't allow her mind to pursue that thought any further.

The waitress repeated the order and wrote it down on her pad before turning away. Realising her concentration was shot, Rory looked between her computer and the girl at the other table. She stared off past the girl and onto the street outside through the front window. A couple of bike riders passed by followed by a woman draped in cheap dollar-store jewellery. That actually summed up this part of Melbourne perfectly, incredibly eclectic with enough health nuts running around that organic food stores did really well on this strip. It made Rory smile despite herself.

"You have a nice smile."

Rory started. No longer reading her book, the stranger met Rory's eyes again in an unapologetic way that dared Rory to look away without acknowledging her.

"Thanks." Rory bit her lip in an attempt to keep herself from looking away. She didn't really know how to handle compliments, especially compliments from striking, dark haired women who wore glasses like the bad girl from *Orange is the New Black*.

The other girl nodded her head as though Rory's reaction had answered something she'd wondered. "I'm Michelle," she said, holding out the hand that didn't have her purse in it.

Rory noted in the seconds before she reached up for Michelle's hand the way her nails were filed, perfectly rounded and painted, evidence of a recent manicure. "Rory," she answered.

"Nice to meet you," Michelle said, sliding her fingers away. Her gaze left Rory as she reached into her purse and pulled out a fifty-dollar note. Kismet was a pay-as-you-feel venue, running off the idea that everyone deserved a seat at the table, even if they couldn't afford more typical eat out options. Michelle's fingers dropped the note into the donation box, before she looked back at Rory again. "Maybe I'll see you around again."

~~*

Coming back to Kismet gave Rory a place to

go in evenings no longer spent partying. She packed her bag every morning with books, her laptop and everything else she needed for the day. Like a sanitary pad.

And then, after a couple of weeks and at the end of the month, it came. Rory cried out before remembering her housemate was home. It hardly mattered to her sense of relief. That was it. She wasn't pregnant. It actually was going to be fine. It was going to be fine.

And she seriously wanted to pop a bottle of champagne to celebrate. Thankfully, there was none in the house.

Helena was reading in the living room as Rory came out.

"Everything okay?" she asked.

"Just got my period. It was late," Rory replied by way of explanation.

She and Helena had first met in first year and decided to go halves in a share house not too far from the campus eighteen months later. They lived well together. Neither of them was especially prone to mess and they weren't dear enough friends that the close proximity of living together grated on either of them. They now lived in an old, rundown two-bedroom unit that had concrete for a backyard and no front yard.

"Ah. So, do you have a new boyfriend?" Helena was a redhead with freckles over her face so thick that she was self-conscious of them whenever they were mentioned. She could have been a cover model had she had more self-confidence, a comment that Rory had only made once before she realised how unwelcome it was.

Rory broke eye contact, turning her face away. She'd been relieved enough that she wasn't pregnant that the thought of the rape hadn't entered her mind until then. "No," she said heavily.

"I just thought that was the reason I hardly ever see you anymore. It's not like you've got classes this morning." Helena shrugged but didn't ask any further questions. Rory's answer hadn't exactly opened up more conversation. Without a promise of some new gossip, Helena went back to painting her nails in relative disinterest.

Rory shoved the last of her stuff into her bag and zipped it closed. It took some doing to heft it up onto her shoulder. She'd end up stronger for it if she kept this up. Before the left the house, she paused, unsure whether she ought to say something else to her housemate. Nothing came to mind, so she stood there kind of awkwardly until Helena looked up at her again.

"I guess I'll see you when I see you," Rory said.
"Yeah…"

Rory left. Her car was parked not too far from where she lived, but it was a nightmare driving up High Street, which was a shared thoroughfare by both cars and trams, and Rory almost always elected the public transport option. Plus, with her student card, it was the far cheaper option.

The tram dinged loudly to advise cars that the doors were about to open and Rory hurried onto it. Melbourne in the middle of the day on a Saturday wasn't too busy, unless one was heading into the heart of the city, so Rory was able to grab a window seat. Across from her sat a mother with a baby on her lap and a boy who was swinging with the rhythm of the moving tram, no matter how often his mum told him to sit down.

Of she, the baby and the mum, the baby seemed like they were the calmest. Rory met the child's eyes. They couldn't have been much more than one year old. Rory was struck by the innocence of this baby who hadn't even learned to talk and was able to have a comfortable interaction with a stranger. Their mum was there to protect them.

Rory had been close to her own mum, Daphne, before all this started. But now she was too embarrassed to even start a conversation with her. She was sure that she wouldn't be able to hide what was going on—her mum had always had a knack of getting under things where her only daughter was concerned—and Rory wasn't sure she was capable of lying to her.

Their last dinner together had been a disaster. It might not have been the case from where Daphne was sitting, but it certainly felt that way for Rory. She'd spent the whole movie trying to figure out if she saw her mum looking curiously her way or whether it was just her imagination.

She was needlessly fidgety until she noticed it, and then self-conscious about her fidgeting. When she tried to plant her hands firmly in her lap, that only made the nervous energy come out of her feet, which then kept up a regular tapping throughout the film.

"Are you sure you're okay?" her mum asked as they were hugged their goodbyes.

Rory had opened her mouth and closed it several times, before saying, "I'm fine. Why wouldn't I be?"

"If you say so," Daphne said, gazing at her doubtfully. "Just remember I'm here if you need me."

In some ways, that made it worse. Rory knew that was her mum's way of saying that she wouldn't bring it up again since Rory didn't want her to. And so Rory had been avoiding out of her growing sense of guilt, only replying to text messages so Daphne wouldn't worry.

At just after eleven a.m., the lunch crowd hadn't yet arrived at Kismet. It was easy to get her standard table in the corner. Because it was the weekend, Rory gave herself permission to start with reading something recreational. With her new routine, there would be more than enough time to get the last of her assignments finished and handed in.

She hadn't been paying attention to the clock, and so didn't know how long she'd been sitting there when someone pulled out a chair in front of her and sat down. That by itself wasn't uncommon in this particular restaurant, though usually the other person asked first. Rory lifted her gaze.

It was the glasses that made her remember who she was staring at. Then the smile. She remembered the smile and the way that it seemed as though she was smiling at some secret only she understood. The loose, black hair and dark-rimmed glasses were the same as the last time.

"May I sit here?" the other girl asked, although the chair was already drawn out.

Rory waved a hand in assent. "I'm sorry, I've completely forgotten your name," she said, flushing with embarrassment.

"Michelle," she reminded her as she sat. "Have you ordered lunch yet?"

Rory shook her head. It had been before the lunch shift had started when she first sat down, so there was only the remains of her coffee on the table with them.

"What are you reading?"

Oh, and the book. That was the other thing on the table. Rory had flipped it down onto its front cover when Michelle had come to sit down. Only the blurb on the back was visible.

"It's about wizards. Sort of like if *Harry Potter* was written from Voldemort's point of view." Rory couldn't help but watch Michelle's reaction closely to figure out whether she was the type to judge. Rory was used to friends at parties mocking her for reading what they deemed 'kids' books'.

Michelle didn't react like that at all. "That sounds really interesting." Reaching past the empty coffee mug, Michelle picked up the book and turned it over in her hands.

Again, Rory noticed the manicured look of Michelle's nails. Different from Helena, who painted her nails with tacky, florescent greens and oranges, Michelle's looked like the hands of an adult.

Rory's phone rang. It started vibrating against the table, drawing both her and Michelle's gazes to it. "Sorry," Rory murmured.

It was her mum. Rory was of two minds about answering it, but Michelle had already seen the phone ringing. It would probably seem weird if she just cancelled the call.

"Excuse me," she said. "Hi, Mum. Actually, I'm out with someone at the moment. Yeah. I can call you back. No worries. Bye."

In front of her, Michelle had already cracked open the start of her book and began to read it.

Rory subtly turned her phone on silent then said to her, "You don't have to do that."

"Do what?" One of Michelle's eyebrows lifted. She looked genuinely curious.

"Seem interested," Rory said quietly. "I know it's kids' stuff."

"Lots of people like reading 'kids' stuff'," Michelle said, turning her attention from the defensive Rory back to the book. "I know I do."

Maybe it was because Michelle was paying more attention to the book than Rory when she said it, but Rory found that she believed it and accepted it. Rory didn't realise until then just how much the people she used to hang around with fed into her insecurities.

"My mum used to read to me," she said, still feeling a need to make an explanation, and since her mum's phone call had stayed on her mind. Having Michelle there to distract her from putting Daphne off again was incredibly welcome. "*Harry Potter* first, but then other stuff. A little bit of Enid Blyton, Tamora Pierce."

Michelle looked up from the book, which she closed and set lightly on the table. Her full attention was on Rory. She really did look interested.

"Before I knew it," Rory said, "that was the kind of thing I was borrowing out of the library."

The corners of Michelle's eyes crinkled behind her glasses, but Rory judged there was something else there as well. "There was never a lot of reading at my home," Michelle admitted, quietly.

"What?" Rory could hardly imagine not a lot of reading. Before alcohol, books had been her only addiction. "I mean, even when you were little?"

Michelle gave a shrug. "I mean, a little, but… I'm the youngest after three boys. None of them liked to read. I think my parents just… assumed." The way she said it said it didn't matter, or that she'd long since made peace with it. "I come to places like this to read sometimes."

"Me too." The smile from before came back to Rory's features.

Then she gave a little happy sound of surprise when Michelle pulled out a book from her own bag. No further words were needed. High Street and Kismet and the customers and wait staff around them vanished. They each comfortably understood that they could quietly read in each other's company until their meals arrived.

After they began to eat, Rory realised that Michelle was listening in to the conversations happening around them. At the same time as the table to their left laughed, a small quirk would appear on Michelle's lips. Likewise when a couple at a table had one of them calling out the other's name in a less than impressed way.

Rory found her own lips quirking in response. She couldn't help it; Michelle's amusement was infectious. Michelle met her eyes, and the two girls burst into laughter that had the couple and the girls at the table to the left of them looking in their direction.

They went back to their reading through the rest of the lunch shift and into Rory's post-meal hot chocolate and Michelle's chai latte. Rory didn't notice that one of the waiters she knew was starting to look at them indulgently as they ignored each other in favour of their books.

Just shy of dinnertime, Michelle closed her

book and set it down on the table. Rory lifted her gaze from the page at the other woman's movement.

"I hoped I'd see you again," Michelle said, as the waiter walked away. "Of course, I was hoping you'd remember my name. But then, I also didn't figure we'd have so much fun in silence."

She spoke the words in a self-deprecating way that could only be taken as a joke. All the same, Rory turned a bit bashful. "It has been great," she said, hoping that Michelle hadn't been bored but polite about it. She knew that she wasn't supposed to be starting any new relationships right now. Not for a year after being sober. That was what all the information said.

Rory met Michelle's eyes. Surely this couldn't be construed as starting a new relationship. As Michelle had just said: they'd just sat together in silence.

Michelle looked into Rory's face as though she wanted to say something. A small smile—a smirk, really, Rory decided on further reflection—lifted the corners of her mouth, before she turned away to reach for something in her bag. Seeming to decide on something, she said, "It's getting late and I don't have any plans tonight. What are you up to?"

"Nothing," Rory said slowly, because it was better than answering; she'd been planning on staying here until they kicked her out.

"Excellent. How would you feel about

continuing this in a place with couches and carpet?" Michelle asked.

"I think I would feel… very good about that." Again, Rory was careful not to sound too desperate for the reprieve.

Again, Michelle put a large amount of money into the pay-as-you-feel donation box, making Rory immediately feel guilty about what she as a student would manage to scrape together by comparison. But Michelle waved her hand at Rory as she reached into her bag. "I covered it for both of us," she said.

Michelle directed them to where she'd parked her car. Rory didn't know anything about cars other than her own, but Michelle's was a black four seater with two doors and chairs that pitched forward in order for a person to get to the backseat. She was glad for the decision to take the tram up from uni.

Traffic was a little busier now that people were heading out for their Saturday night plans. Rory focused on the interior of the car rather than note how many bars they drove past before Michelle turned down a side street. The way was slow going as Michelle drove in the direction of the city, along with the flow of the rest of the traffic, but it was only a suburb or two until Michelle pulled into her driveway.

It was fairly late in the twilight, and Rory could hear a few crickets in the grass nearby. But the inner suburb townhouse was not in an area where there was a lot of grass or trees. Only one tree stood in front of Michelle's house, and almost all of its leaves had already fallen off.

Rory tried not to appear too surprised by the neat looking townhouse they drew up into. Maybe she'd become too used to the deteriorating student housing and cheap units where parties were held. Rory looked at her companion with new eyes when she realised it had been hours since the last time she'd thought about the party she was missing right now. Of course, the book had had something to do with it, too. But Michelle had made it fun.

Michelle showed her in through the hall to the open plan kitchen and living room area. There was an L shaped couch in the corner, opposite a TV that Michelle turned on immediately via remote to play digital radio.

"Please, sit," Michelle told her, before moving around the room to turn on various lamps and the kettle.

Rory did as she was told. She felt rude pulling out her book and reading while Michelle still wandered around.

"Can I get you a drink?" Michelle asked. She'd pulled out mugs already.

"Just water, thanks," Rory said gratefully. "I can get it…" And anyway, it gave her something to do while Michelle continued to putter.

The two girls moved comfortably together in the kitchen, not bumping into each other or getting in each other's way. When the kettle boiled, Michelle poured herself a cup of tea, then both of them headed back to the couch. Michelle's hands warmed around the drink, her bare feet lifted up onto the couch. The music from the digital radio—mellow at this time of evening—swirled around them.

"So," Rory said, lifting her mug up to her lips and sipping the water, "Do you often invite people to your house to ignore them while reading?"

"Sometimes," Michelle answered equitably. Her eyes widened and danced with mischief. "Sometimes I even talk to them."

Rory gasped, joining in the gentle mockery easily. "Say it isn't so!"

"It is," Michelle added, ruefully. "Sometimes they talk back. That's when it gets really messy. Conversations can start that way."

"So I've heard." Rory nodded sagely. Her book was behind her on the couch where she'd left it when she attempted to help Michelle in the kitchen. Now her body tilted towards Michelle, her book all but forgotten. She narrowed her gaze, eyeing Michelle, considering. "Do we dare venture into that territory?"

Michelle laughed. Her head tilted back and she sounded as if she let the joy out freely. "Oh, my dear," she said, and Rory chuckled at how pretentious they both sounded. "I fear we already have."

Instead of conversing about having a conversation, conversation moved to how long Michelle had had this house, its proximity to her work, her favourite shops nearby. Much less than engaging in small talk with the other woman, Rory found she was actually interested in hearing Michelle's answers, watching the way her body moved as she gesticulated an answer or looked off into the middle distance while considering something she was about to say or had just said.

"Enough about me." Michelle put her empty tea mug down and pinned Rory with a stare. "I want to know about you."

Rory gazed at Michelle a little bit warily. "What do you want to know?"

"Well, so far, I know you enjoy reading books," Michelle said playfully. She leaned her back against the back of the couch, merely watching Rory where she had been animated before. "So I'd say pretty much anything. What are you studying?"

Rory gave a short laugh under her breath. "I've watched peoples' eyes glaze over when I talk to them about this," she warned.

"Try me," Michelle dared.

"I study sociology, with a specific focus on feudalism." It was the quickest way to go about explaining. People could opt out at the point if they wanted to, and Rory wasn't left with the feeling that she was as boring.

"Oh." Michelle's expression was perfectly

pleasant as that one syllable articulated aptly that she had no knowledge at all on the subject. Rory was grateful that she didn't ask some random question to do with the study just for no other reason than politeness. Instead, she said, "That's a really... random interest."

"It really is," Rory said with a grin. "It comes from my 'I want to be an archaeologist' days."

Michelle leaned back against the couch, bringing a hand just below her mouth in a way that really drew Rory attention to her lips. "What happened?" she murmured.

Rory hesitated a moment, trying to think of something witty that might not betray how distracted she'd suddenly become. "Too many dusty old corpses." A pause. "They wore tweed and taught archaeology."

Michelle gave a laugh, and it rang out clearly through the room in a way that had Rory smiling with her. "And here I imagined you as a womanly Indiana Jones."

"Not even close." Rory chuckled. "I liked sociology more. It's more of about what's going on behind the scenes sort of study. Turned out I wasn't an archaeologist after all."

"Probably for the best that you found that out sooner rather than later."

"Probably," Rory said, with another laugh. "So what about you? What's your day job?"

"Ah." Again, that hand moved very close to Michelle's lips. Rory's gaze followed it. "I'm afraid

I'm nowhere near as interesting as I appear."

"I'm sure that's not true," Rory protested mildly.

She smiled. "I'm a personal assistant in a freight forwarding company. Nothing incredibly exciting."

"That does sound interesting. A personal assistant!"

"Honestly, it's just a lot of wandering around, making sure all the higher ups have everything they need on a daily basis." She shrugged. "And yet, I'm happy where I am. I could comfortably stay in that job for the next twenty years."

"Wow." Rory couldn't quite imagine doing any one thing for the next twenty years. "It must be really nice to have that kind of job security so young."

Michelle's eyebrows rose. "How young do you think I am?"

"I dunno…" Rory bit her lip. Not for the first time that day, a feeling of insecurity washed over her. She really hated this question; there was no right way to answer it. She thought about her own age, and guessed Michelle was at least a couple of years older. "Mid-twenties?" she guessed.

"Try 29," Michelle answered. Then, seeing Rory's shock, she added, "Thank you, though. I'll take the compliment."

"You should! Does it… bother you that I'm 22?"

"Why would it bother me?"

Why indeed. Rory could think of at least half a dozen things that were likely to bother her more.

And then Rory yawned. She didn't mean to. She was enjoying this conversation and time with Michelle more than she'd expected. Her eyes widened even as her mouth refused to shut.

"Oh god, I'm not bored talking to you!" Rory said, mortified. "I'm not even that tired, really. I'm enjoying this."

"I am, too." Michelle smiled warmly, but Rory noticed for the first time that Michelle's lack of movement against the back of the couch looked more like tiredness now than restraint. "And I've got heaps more questions. But…"

"It's late," Rory finished for her.

Michelle inclined her head.

"I should be going."

"Do you want me to give you a lift?"

But Rory looked at the way Michelle didn't even prop herself up against the couch as she said it. She smiled, for the offer was nice even if she felt a need to decline it. "It's honestly not hard to get back home from here. Just a tram down to Bundoora."

"Will you text me when you get home?" At this question, Michelle just raised one delicately plucked eyebrow over the rim of her glasses.

Rory didn't know why, but the question sounded far more salacious than it should have done. "I'll probably need your number."

"Hand me your phone," she said.

While Michelle keyed her number into Rory's mobile, Rory watched the sharp, slender fingers moving quickly across the screen. There was a knowing look in Michelle's gaze as she handed the phone back to Rory.

"I hope you'll come back soon."

Rory met Michelle's eyes. Michelle wasn't kicking her out, and Rory hadn't misread Michelle's interest. The awareness of it caused a small smile to bloom on her lips.

"I will," she promised. "Sleep well."

Chapter Three

It was late when Rory shoved the key into her front door.

The light immediately revealed Tally, sitting in the middle of her couch in the living room. Tally was one of the girls she'd most often partied and gotten drunk with in the past. For a second, Rory couldn't say anything, unable to reconcile past and present together.

"What? What are you—?" The words came out like staccato bullets. She didn't know what she was trying to say. It was just too harsh a juxtaposition against her time with Michelle.

"Helena said I could wait for you." Tally stood up slowly, smoothing her hands over her knee length skirt.

Just the sight of her made Rory feel like she was dangerously close to slip-sliding backwards. If she could just deflect Tally, make her answer more of her questions than she answered, then things could stay on an even keel.

The banging against the inside of her chest told her that she was lying to herself.

"Why aren't you out partying?" Rory said, trying to continue through with her plan all the same. It was the only thing she had to hold onto.

"It's not the same without you." Tally moved to stand in front of her. The door was a little bit open behind Rory. She'd barely taken two steps into the room when she'd first seen Tally. Now she deliberately kept the door open so that she didn't feel trapped. Rory could leave at any time, even if this was her home.

"You need to go," Rory said. All questions fled out of her mind as she broke eye contact and stared unsteadily at the floor. Nothing else was going to work. Tally needed to leave now. She should never have been allowed to come in!

"Why?" There was a smile in Tally's voice, but Rory had heard it before. She knew it was accompanied by a hard look in the other girl's eyes. "You have assignments due? Not feeling well? I hope you have a doctor's note for that, Aurora."

"Don't," Rory said weakly.

Tally lifted both hands as though making peace. "I'm sorry. I didn't mean to. Look, I know you've been busy. But I miss you. And it's not like you've made it easy to get a hold of you and see how you're doing. You never seem to be out anywhere anymore." Both Tally's voice and face looked younger as she made that admission.

Rory opened her mouth and closed it again. She hadn't even considered how Tally would feel about her sudden disappearance. Abandoned, Rory realised, and hurt. Hurt enough to lash out? Rory put that thought aside as paranoid. She didn't even know Tally all that well. Enough that they'd kissed a couple of times at parties, but nothing else. Not that Rory could remember anyway.

"Smithy was worried he'd done something," Tally continued, talking about her boyfriend now. "I told him he hadn't, but I didn't have much to go on, you know?"

"Smithy didn't do anything," Rory said through numb lips. Smithy had been kind to her. She actually knew him better than she knew Tally. She started to say, *None of you did*, but then the hazy, fragmented images of waking up with that strange guy mouthing off at her, and then waking up in bed with Tally and some other dude came back to her, and she couldn't quite work her mouth around the words. Maybe she and Tally had done more than kiss a couple of times. Rory just didn't know, and she didn't dare ask. It would be better for everyone if she could just be left to forget about all of it.

Tally nodded once, and then it was like she was done being hurt or something. "Look, I won't stay long. I just wanted… Fuck, I dunno, I just wanted to make sure you were okay. You've been too busy to party, so I thought I'd bring the party to you."

As Tally stepped aside, Rory saw it on the couch behind her. A bottle of Champagne with a pastel pink bow around the neck.

"I figured by now you would have finished

and handed in at least one of your assignments, so, celebration," Tally said, following Rory's line of sight. There was a hint of uncertainty in Tally's voice, and that was the reason why Rory couldn't throw her out. Tally's eyes looked shadowed, as though she hadn't been getting enough sleep. Her hair looked lanky. Most of all, now that the hard look was gone, Tally looked sad. Lonely, even.

Rory let out a shuddering breath as she glanced between friend and alcohol. She didn't want to come any further into the room, closer to the temptation. Yet she couldn't help herself. She was merely a good hostess—Rory told herself—*that* was what drew her across the room to find two cups in the cupboard where she and Helena kept them.

"Just one glass," she said to herself, to Tally, not quite looking at her friend as she poured.

Tally relaxed perceptibly. "Whatever you want," she said before grinning at Rory and reaching for her glass.

Just like that, the two girls slid back into comfortable back and forth wit and banter, with neither one of them addressing any further reasons Rory had stopped going out to parties.

They drank more than one glass each.

When the bottle was empty, Tally tipped it over with her foot as she stood up to join Rory in the bed.

~~*

Rory woke up with a dry, fuzzy feeling in the back of her throat and recognised it immediately.

"No…" she murmured. She closed her eyes again, hardly able to believe that this had happened. That she had let this happen. Again. But that only brought her face to face with her own thoughts and hangover.

She pushed herself out of bed to the sound of Tally's half asleep, "Mmmph?" Rory ignored that as she grabbled for her phone and stumbled towards bathroom.

Pressing her hands against the sink, Rory tried not to hyperventilate. Looking up into the mirror was worse—the sight of her bedraggled hair and washed out lips—so she trained her eyes down on the spaces between her fingers.

"It'll be all right. It's gonna be all right." She whispered it under her breath, trying to put strength and belief into the sounds. She closed her eyes and mouthed the words, but flashes of the night before came vividly to the backs of her eyelids. The fact that she hadn't blacked out wasn't a comfort.

Rory closed her eyes and shook her head. Tears seeped through her closed eyes to trail down her cheeks. It was only then that she heard the sound of footsteps outside the door.

"Rory?" It was a soft query at first, followed by a soft tapping of fingernails on the locked door. "Are you okay?"

Tally. Inside the bathroom, Rory shook her head, but when she called out it was to say, "I'm fine." Her voice was muffled, and the result of trying to stifle crying had blocked her nose, but the words came out clear enough.

There was a pause, but then the footsteps walked away.

Rory couldn't leave the bathroom. She couldn't face Tally. Not now. Not ever.

Even as muddled as she was currently feeling, she knew she couldn't hide all day. Helena would be back soon, and she didn't want to worry her housemate. Rory needed to pull herself together.

It wasn't going to be all right. She didn't know how to make it all right.

When she shakily opened the bathroom again, Tally was sitting up in Rory's bed, and wiping her eyes. "I just wondered where you went," she said, blinking up at the other girl sleepily. "Are you okay?"

"You need to leave. Now. Please," Rory added as an afterthought. She didn't care if she came across as rude. She could barely look at Tally and that wasn't about to change if they had a nice conversation together now.

Tally woke up enough to realise that something was really wrong here. "What's up?" she asked. A line appeared between her eyebrows.

Rory closed her eyes and tried counting to three; tried not to take this out on Tally. "I just really don't think…" She shook her head. There was no way to articulate the thought out loud without coming across as insulting. "I just feel a little bit—"

"Sick," Tally said, misinterpreting what Rory was trying to say and wording it better than Rory could have hoped. Then Rory realised that she hadn't been so lucky with Tally's next words. "I'm getting used to it. Why don't you give me a call when you get better." She picked up the bag that had been abandoned on the floor the night before, pulled on boots with rough, jerky movements, then stomped to the door and slammed it behind her.

Rory lifted her gaze briefly to the space Tally had passed through. Then she covered her face and sobbed into her hands.

~~*

It was her only second time coming to the AA group. She knew she should have been coming more regularly. Maybe it wasn't such a surprise that she'd fallen at the first hurdle. If she'd taken these meetings more seriously, attended them regularly, maybe things would have been different.

She blamed herself.
She blamed Tally.
She blamed herself.
It was the same setting as the first time. The

wheelchair ramp was lit by a porch light as it was getting darker earlier now that Melbourne was settling into winter weather. The trees along the street were as bare as the one outside of Michelle's house. Rory frowned. She didn't want to think about Michelle here. That was just one more person she wanted to hide this mess from.

Some of the people gathered around the room she recognised from the last time, but there were new people too. The facilitators, she found out, worked on a rotating schedule as well, so they were two more people she didn't recognise.

She found the lack of people who recognised *her* strangely reassuring and wondered if that was wrong.

Rory didn't speak as much as she had in the first session, but did speak in answer to a few stories in the first half of the session. During the break at 8:30, she found herself in conversation with the only girl there who was clearly younger than her.

"Did your mum drive you here too?" The young girl's face was painted, strips of black across the eyes, red across the lips, and bronze across the cheeks, adding definition to her features. She wanted look older. The girl hadn't spoken up in the meeting, so this was the first time Rory heard her clipped, brash voice. Her arms were crossed across her slim chest, head tipped to the side.

"Um. No." Rory swallowed, giving a quick

glance around the tea room to see how many people might overhear their conversation. "My mum doesn't know I'm here." She still hadn't called Daphne back, despite the fact that guilt made it harder and harder every day. Daphne hadn't called back again either.

"Lucky you," said the teen, completely missing the direction of Rory's thoughts. The toilet flushed and the bathroom door opened. The younger girl abandoned Rory in favour of the bathroom.

"My family doesn't know about this either." It was the balding man she'd talked to before. Rory wondered which family—his parents, or the wife and children he'd lost?—but it didn't seem polite to ask.

"I don't want to worry her," Rory said, quieter than when she'd spoken to the young girl. "My mum," she clarified. "I don't want her to think this is more serious than it is."

The man gave her a sad smile, and then soon after they were brought back into the larger room for the second half of the meeting.

Rory thought over her words and the sad look from the balding man as other people spoke for the next hour. She didn't want her mum to think this was more serious than it was. How serious, exactly, did Rory think this problem was? On the one hand, she still managed to stay on top of all her uni work; more so now that she was pouring all her dedication to stay away from alcohol into her assignments. But it was also serious enough that she'd been staying away from alcohol; that she was here.

That she'd almost wanted to vomit from fear and guilt and repulsion on Sunday morning.

And then there was the silence between people sharing their stories, and Rory decided to speak.

"I drank again on Saturday night." There was a rumbling of commiseration and understanding around the room. Rory met the eyes of the bald man long enough to see that the sad expression was in his gaze again. "A friend came over with a bottle of champagne. I didn't black out, but... I woke up the next morning and I felt..." Rory shook her head slowly. She didn't know how to verbalise how she had felt the following morning, waking up with a headache from half a bottle of champagne, and with the knowledge something very wrong had happened to her.

"I felt so angry at her, at my friend," Rory continued. "Like, how dare she come over to my place? I would have been fine if she hadn't. But I know that wasn't right. I've been hiding this from my mum because I don't want to worry her, because I don't want to disappoint her. I haven't told anyone about this. I have this idea that I'll fix this on my own, and then I won't need to mention it. That's why drinking again was so hard. I felt like I was going right back to the start, completely out of control."

There was a respectful silence for a moment after she shared. Then someone she didn't know spoke up. "I think we've all felt that way. I have. Some people seek the feeling out of control that alcohol gives us and are excited by it. It sounds, at least, like that's not the case with you."

Rory shook her head vehemently. "No! It's not," she agreed.

"There are always going to be situations like that," a middle-aged woman, said. "Alcohol and drinking is just part of our culture. What we need to do is learn how to say 'no'."

Rory tried to imagine herself going back to that room, and Tally, and the bottle of champagne, and saying 'no'. In the moment, it had been something that was completely unimaginable. She hadn't wanted Tally to get angry with her. But then, the next day when she'd asked Tally to leave, the other girl had gotten angry with her anyway. Rory sighed, feeling defeated.

"How do I do that without someone else getting angry at me?" Rory asked in a very small voice. The girl who'd been driven here by her mum snorted. While Rory tried to ignore it, it was also so close to exactly what she was afraid of that she winced before saying, "I don't really have any friends who don't drink."

"Perhaps," said the first guy who spoke, "it's time to get new friends."

~~*

When she got home that night, she started her

computer and pulled up the people she'd friended. The majority of people listed there were people whom she'd friended or had friended her over the years of piss up parties. Most of them she didn't even know very well.

Those were the easiest ones to defriend.

Rory tried not to think of people trying to contact her and finding out that she'd defriended them; she tried to take this thing one step at a time, but it was hard. She imagined Tally storming up to her place again to demand answers, knowing exactly where she lived and Helena inviting her to wait for her in all over again.

Her phone rang. Rory jumped, thinking that Tally must have been online and already seen what she'd done. Her heart was still pounding when she saw that it was her mum.

Dread curled in her stomach, a different feeling from the actual fear she exhibited at the idea of interacting with Tally again.

"Hello?"

"Darling. Are you okay? Your voice sounds a little funny."

Between her stomach and her pounding heart, Rory was surprised that her voice only sounded a little funny. "You caught me on my way to the library," she lied. "Apparently, I'm a little unfit."

Her mum chuckled down the phone line, and the dread in her stomach curled a little bit tighter.

"Actually, can I call you back? I'm just in the middle of planning an essay in my head, and I don't want to lose the idea."

"Of course, darling." Her mum was graceful enough not to comment on the fact that Rory had said she'd call before and hadn't. "While I've got you, I just meant to ask: Are you free at any time this week for dinner?"

"No," Rory said quickly. "I'm just swamped. Mid-term assessments are all due in."

"Ah, well that's what you've got to do first. But if you happen to get ahead of them…" Daphne said.

"You'll be the first one to know. Love you, Mum. Gotta go." Rory got off the phone. She considered turning it off, but settled for putting it on silent and stuffing it in the bottom of her bag.

She got back onto her computer, finished saving her new social media settings, then turned the computer off and tried to get some sleep.

Chapter Four

Rory didn't regret exchanging numbers with Michelle. She was, in fact, incredibly glad when the text messages became a light, regular distraction and part of her days.

I kind of miss being at uni. At least then when I was this bored, I was sitting in the midst of 100 other people and could zone out. These people *pay* me to act like I'm impressed.

Rory smirked. As Michelle had pointed out, it wasn't as though the lecturer would notice one of one hundred students texting in the middle of the lecture hall. She kept her arm low as she made her reply, not wanting to come across as too obvious. *Trade places with you. right now it seems like Im about to die of boredom.*

Michelle's quick reply was a smiley face.

Her next message came later in the day, after the lecture was finished and while Rory was in the library.

Big window offices are distracting. I need to work, not stare out into the sunshine!

ah, Rory wrote in reply. *i think you've just uncovered the real reason why there's so little lighting in libraries.*

No, no. That's there to protect the books.

It was times like this, when Michelle said or wrote things like that, that Rory realised Michelle was really smart.

What are you reading? was the rest of her text.

Histories and law of feudal Europe, Rory replied. *its very exciting stuff.*

Rory packed up her things as the lights in the library began to go off, indicating it was closing. She didn't have anything to borrow, so she went straight to the front doors.

"Oh, sorry!" she said reflexively when her bag bumped against someone else.

"Hey, that's okay," Smithy said. His lips turned in a surprised but friendly smile. "It's good to see you again. I was beginning to wonder if you'd dropped out."

Rory struggled to keep the smile on her face all of a sudden. "Oh, uh, yeah. I've just been really busy." It was strange that Tally hadn't mentioned seeing her. Instead of saying more, she continued forward, moving through the sensors checking for barcodes of books that hadn't been borrowed out.

"Yeah." Smithy wandered through with her. "I heard that," he said, which might have indicated talking to Tally after all. Rory already felt hopelessly out of her depth in this conversation, and they'd hardly made it past the pleasantries.

He fell into step with her. He was much taller than her, so he must have shortened his stride to not rush off ahead of her. It was different than seeing Tally in her home, in her space.

Intimidating still, but less so. She just hoped he wasn't about to pull out a hip flask.

"You don't have to walk with me," she said, giving him explicit permission to leave.

"I don't mind," he replied.

Rory bit her lip, not sure what she was meant to say next. She considered trying to pretend like he wasn't there or was just another completely isolated student simply using the same walking path as her, but that didn't work with his mass and expectation of a conversation. Her lips were already bitten ragged from stress and recriminations. It had been far harder to stay away from alcohol this week than it'd been the week before. She couldn't have smiled at Smithy right now even if she'd wanted to without splitting her lip in at least two places.

That didn't seem to matter to Smithy. He was smiling enough for both of them, as he looked down towards her. There seemed no indication in his expression that he was aware of her defriending him online. But would there be even if he did know?

Rory's hands were stuffed deep in her pockets, shoulders hunched defensively. She tried to straighten them, so she wasn't quite so transparent. She felt uncomfortable and miserable. He was too much of a reminder of everything she'd done wrong. Her brain didn't seem to care that it wasn't his fault.

She couldn't take the pressure. They'd only

walked about 400 metres when Rory stopped dead in the middle of their path. As late as it was, there wasn't a problem with anyone oncoming, and it didn't take Smithy more than a step to notice and stop.

"I can't," Rory said. "Whatever you're thinking, whatever we've done, whatever I promised, I can't, okay?"

"Done?" Smithy asked. His brows furrowed, and he actually looked concerned. That made things worse! It wasn't the way she'd expected the conversation to go in her head. She was breathing too fast. She needed to say something. The silence after he spoke went on too long.

"Exactly." Okay, that didn't make much sense, but Rory pushed on. "I'm trying to do something here. It's why I haven't been around you or Tally or anyone else for a while. I'd appreciate it if you would just accept that. Tell people if you need to; I don't care."

"I'm sorry if I've done anything at all that made you uncomfortable." A furrow between his brows, he held his hands up in surrender, looking like a big, friendly giant. He was genuinely worried—Rory could see that plainly—and it took her out of her head for just a bit. She didn't like what she saw, what she was causing.

Rory wanted to cry. "It's not you. It's me. It's…" But she didn't want to talk to him. As kind and concerned and confused as he appeared, he was still Tally's boyfriend. There was no way that this strange interaction between the two of them wasn't going to make its way back to Tally, and Tally was one of the people she most wanted to avoid, right now. "Just, believe me, okay? I'm not great to be around."

The confusion in his expression turned to hurt. Rory hated that hurt expression. It seemed like she caused it with everyone she talked to lately. They'd both stopped walking, and Rory wondered if she could get away with just walking again and leaving him behind.

"But how do I do that without someone else getting angry at me?"

"Perhaps it's time to get new friends."

Rory hardened her heart. She was working on it. She knew that the AA group wasn't meant to take the place of counselling, but what that guy had said made sense to her. So what if Smithy was a real and genuine guy who she'd always enjoyed talking to, drunk or sober? He was part of a crowd she couldn't be around right now. That had to come first.

Smithy was trying to find his words again. "Okay, it seems like I've upset you. It wasn't my intention…"

"No," Rory said, tired all of a sudden. "It's my fault. Like I said, I'm going through something right now. I'm just gonna go home now, okay? On my own."

She quickened her pace before Smithy could join her again. Only just barely did she manage to refrain from looking around to see whether Smithy was following her.

When she got back home, she found Helena in the living room, wearing headphones and looking at something on her computer. She spared a wave in Rory's direction but otherwise ignored her. Rory was glad for it. It was the first time she'd seen her since she'd invited Tally in to wait for her. She needed to tell her not to do that again but, after seeing Smithy, her emotions were too close to the surface. Rory couldn't deal with another confrontation right now.

Instead, she ducked into her bedroom, slumped onto her bed, and pulled her phone out of her pocket. There were no new messages from Michelle, so she started a new one.

Im so glad to be able to text you. sometimes it feels like all the people I know at uni are crazy.

Or she was, Rory thought to herself, but she didn't send that bit.

It didn't take that long before there was a reply from Michelle. *Ahh, *that's* the reason I'm glad I'm not at uni anymore.*

There was a moment, then another message appeared.

Are you okay?

Rory started typing out a message she would have written to anyone else. Then she deleted it, and tried again.

Only on the third try did she slow down enough to give Michelle an answer that was true, but also one she was comfortable with sending. *Ive been better honestly. I think I just completely overreacted to a friend of mine.*

Rory sent that, then added, *someone who used to be a friend of mine.*

Sounds serious. Did you want to talk about it? Michelle replied.

For a minute, Rory just felt so comfortable interacting with someone who knew nothing about her life or history before the last week. She cradled her phone in her hands, while the mattress cradled her back. With Helena in her own virtual world in another part of their small home, it was almost like Rory was alone but for Michelle.

not really. but talking just like this helps.

Well. I'll just have to keep messaging you, then.

~~*

The next night, it was around dinnertime and she and Michelle had been messaging since Rory's three p.m. lecture. She'd long since turned the phone off silent as the only person who successfully contacted her was Michelle.

This is ridiculous. Do you want to have dinner with me? Michelle asked.

sure. at Kismet?

I was thinking maybe somewhere a little bit different. Where's the best place to pick you up?

After organising the details, Rory was

standing outside on the nature strip outside of her group of units with her book in hand when a car pulled into the parking lane in front of her. The window slid down and Michelle looked out at her over a pair of sunglasses.

"Feel like going my way?" Michelle said, dropping her voice to a lower than normal register. Her made up lips smirked in a very familiar expression.

"Fancy seeing you here," Rory quipped right back as she opened the passenger door and slipped into the car.

"Wow, it's almost strange to hear your voice in person again." Michelle looked out of the side mirror and over her shoulder before pulling out onto the street.

"It hasn't been *that* long," said Rory, pushing her book into her bag.

"If you say so." There was a smirk on Michelle's lips.

"It's good to see you too." Actually, it was really good. Better than Rory could have expected from just getting out of the university for a little while. She felt giddy and like the weight that had been following her most days this week had finally lifted.

Maybe there was something more in Rory's tone than she meant to express. Michelle looked over to her from her driver's side, but she didn't say anything.

"So where are we going tonight?" Rory asked,

mostly to steer the conversation back towards lighter, less confusing topics.

The restaurant Michelle took them to was further outside the city than where Rory lived. Rory was used to a certain amount of trees and parkland where she lived, but the area Michelle took her to had tall trees lining both sides of the street, almost blocking out glow from the streetlights.

"This is near where I grew up," Michelle said by way of explanation. "It's a hidden treasure."

Rory had to say she was surprised when she pulled up in front of a small strip of shops with many available parking spaces. There was a milk bar, a bottle-o, a Laundromat, and a wood panelled, old style pizzeria. There was a small outside area in front of the pizzeria, but it was starting to get too late in the season, too cold, to do anything other than sit inside.

"It's a hidden treasure?" Rory's question was tongue in cheek and companied with a raised eyebrow.

"I figured you wouldn't judge based on appearances," Michelle said, all faux innocence.

"What, because I'm a uni student?" Rory asked, with mocking offence.

"More or less," Michelle replied, sticking her tongue out.

"Careful, or I'll bite it off!" Rory didn't mean it, not really. It was just difficult to break from the clever banter now they'd started.

Michelle linked arms with Rory as they began to cross the road. "I don't have a problem with that. Although usually I'm the one who's biting."

~~*

The waiter came around to greet them and take their order, and they both looked up from the menus.

"Can I get you a drink?" Michelle asked.

Rory blanched and temporarily lost her words with the waiter standing by the table with a courteous expression, holding the pen and pad in his hands. She just stared into Michelle's face, her whole world narrowing down to the other girl and the table between them.

It seemed like hours later that Michelle turned to the waiter and said, "Just water for us, please."

The waiter nodded and walked away. Rory blinked dry eyes and turned her gaze to the table as Michelle reached out and took her hand.

"What happened?" Her voice was as gentle as the hand touching hers on the table.

"I-I…" Rory started to say, but couldn't figure out how to articulate an explanation. She knew one was owed, and that made her even more tongue-tied. Up till now, the only people she'd talked to about this were the people in the AA group. They were all in the same situation, or similar enough. How she was supposed to bring it up during a night out with Michelle?

As ever, Michelle seemed to recognise something in Rory's expression and the words she didn't say. "The iced tea they have here is very good. There's lemon, of course, but also peach and strawberry."

Rory smiled gratefully at the table, before raising her gaze to look at the other woman. "Strawberry, you say?"

When the waiter next came by, they were ready to order two strawberry iced teas as well as their mains. Although they had glossed over the moment earlier, Rory felt it like a trap that could spring at any moment.

She glanced at a couple nearby who laughed together before sipping from glasses of red and felt like Michelle couldn't fail to know what remained unspoken between them. She felt guilty, like she had misrepresented herself when she started becoming Michelle's friend, like she should have come with a warning label, there was something wrong with her, and she couldn't be treated like a normal person.

Because it *was* totally normal to ask if she wanted a drink. Now that time had passed, and they were both sipping on their iced tea, Rory couldn't help but wonder if this was what Michelle had been meaning all along. Whether it was only Rory who had assumed she'd meant something alcoholic.

When their mains came, it was a relief to have the food in her mouth and have an excuse not to talk. Not to have to check what she said in case it betrayed her guilt. And yet, at the same time, she almost wanted Michelle to find out. That offhand 'biting' comment from the earlier conversation took on a different connotation. She wanted someone to tell her that she was wrong. She should be able to control herself around alcohol. She wanted punishment, as though that could somehow make it better.

"What are you thinking?" Michelle's voice was a delicate prodding, pitched just above the volume of the room. Rory swallowed the mouthful of lamb from her pizza and wondered how much of what she had been thinking had been evident on her face.

"I was thinking of the biting comment you made earlier." Rory twisted her lips. Maybe she could pass it off as flirty.

Michelle's eyebrows arched, interest immediate in her expression. "Oh, you were, were you?"

Rory shrugged. "Well, not many people would say—"

"I'm not 'many people'," Michelle returned, holding her gaze.

For some reason, Rory blushed. Michelle held her gaze a moment longer, before letting her look away. Rory exhaled heavily as her gaze returned to her plate. She'd genuinely had the feeling of Michelle 'letting' her look away. That wasn't a normal thought to have, was it?

When they finished their mains, Michelle asked if she wanted to share a dessert. Rory found it a welcome reprieve. More than 'welcome', if she was honest. Her skin felt flushed. She'd never been out with a girl like this before, at a restaurant, on an actual date. It had been a while since she'd done any of these things with a guy either.

But as Michelle reached over to Rory side of the table, skimming against Rory forearm as she reached for the fork, Rory felt a *zing* that she just didn't remember feeling before. Her heart pounded, and she was pretty sure that she was sweating a little bit. Glowing, her mum would have said, if Rory had told her about this date before it happened.

"So, do you often offer to share a dessert just after articulating a sexual preference?" Rory asked as soon as she was sure that she could say the sentence without squeaking.

"Only with the really special girls," Michelle replied, and Rory found herself blushing again.

"You're way better at this than me," Rory complained.

"Practice," Michelle said lightly, and with a shrug that brought Rory's attention to her shoulders under the thin cardigan she wore.

Again, Rory brain went to the dark place, where the only practice she'd had of interactions like this was kissing Tally while drunk or passing out then waking up wrapped around her.

"I think I need more practice," Rory said. She

struggled to keep her voice even, not wanting to change or lower the mood between them.

"I'd be happy to offer that."

Rory had a strange feeling like they were speaking differing languages and realised she didn't have an easy reference for this kind of flirty banter with another girl without three glasses of whiskey and a couple of beers.

"I'd like that," Rory said slowly, testing out the words as she said them. She dared look back up into Michelle's eyes, cautious and wanting to know if they were still speaking separate languages.

At the end of the night, Michelle paid again.

"I have more disposable income," Michelle said, making it sound completely reasonable before she put her purse away and linked arms with Rory.

By now, their linked arms were almost starting to feel normal. They were closer than they had been before. Rory could feel the heat of Michelle's body, the press of her arm against the curve of breast, and their hips brushing mid step now and then.

They didn't go directly back to the car, but rather a park that had several lights along the path. The cool air felt okay given that they were walking, and Rory didn't think about whether she was cold with Michelle pressed so close.

Michelle stopped walking by a tree and, linked as they were, Rory stopped too.

"May I kiss you?" Michelle asked, and it surprised Rory because she couldn't remember the last time a guy had taken the time to ask instead of assuming.

Her lips curved, and she nodded, not trusting her voice. There was no denying that something was starting between them anymore. Yet, for all that she knew she shouldn't, she was terrible at saying 'no'.

Their first kiss was light, and slow, soft lips moving over each other, nothing so forceful as would encourage the accidental intrusion of teeth. Rory exhaled before opening her eyes as Michelle pulled away first. She looked at Michelle in time to see the other girl reaching a hand up to caress her cheek. Without thinking, Rory leaned into it.

"Mm." The sound rumbled out of Michelle appreciatively. "I love how responsive you are."

Rory was glad for the relative darkness that hid her blush this time.

"I've never…" Rory said shaking her head ever so slightly. "Not with a girl." She didn't want to count any of the times she'd been out of her mind and not able to consent as any of the first times she'd kissed a girl. *This* was the first kiss. She had a choice in that much at least.

Michelle smiled. Either her blushing or her stuttering pleased Michelle as much as her responsiveness; her smirk crept back onto the other girl's lips. Rory couldn't help but be drawn to those lips, the shape of them already so familiar.

"Ah, good. I get to be special too." Her hand drifted away from Rory cheek, and the skin felt cooler there in the absence of the touch. "Come." She offered her hand out this time, and Rory took it. "Let's get you home."

Chapter Five

Rory was almost annoyed by the way she was all but floating through classes the next day. She didn't mean to be one of *those girls*. She didn't *want* to be one of those girls. Just because she'd kissed someone new, didn't mean that it had to change her whole world. Of course, her whole world was recently a lot smaller than it had been at the start of term.

Despite this stern talking to herself, it wasn't until about four p.m. that she came firmly down to earth. She was walking towards the library and looked up from the books she was counting to make sure she'd brought everything she intended to return.

Tally and Smithy were walking towards her. Rory gaze was drawn to their clasped hands as though that part of their joined bodies were magnetised. Another quick glance up told her that there was no way for her to avoid them. They'd already seen her. Tally was walking ahead of Smithy, dragging him along with her by way of their linked hands. This was the first time since defriending everybody and shutting down her privacy settings that Rory had seen Tally. She just couldn't believe that it had gone unnoticed and hunched in on herself warily.

"I knew we'd have to see you here eventually." Tally untangled her hand from Smithy's in order to throw both her arms around Rory. Rory licked suddenly dry lips, unwilling to wrap her arms around Tally with the same enthusiasm. Tally didn't seem to notice. She pulled away and glanced at Smithy. "Didn't I tell you?"

"Yes." By contrast to Tally's over excitement, Smithy seemed reserved. "You did."

Rory wasn't sure if Tally was high, or drunk—it was the middle of the day, but it wasn't completely unreasonable given that it was a Thursday afternoon—or whether she was overcompensating in front of Smithy to act like nothing was wrong.

From the sympathetic look on Smithy's eyes as he gazed at Rory over Tally's shoulder, he knew something was up. His eyebrows were lifted slightly as though he was also still confused about his own recent interaction with Rory. He mouthed something that looked like, *Are you okay?*

Rory looked away.

Unfortunately, that left her back to looking at Tally.

"Have you had dinner yet?" Tally asked, still in the same pushy-light tone of voice.

"Oh, um, no." She lifted the library books that were in her arms, as if they could supply weight to explanation for her. "I still have some—"

At the sudden frown lowering the corners of

Tally's mouth, Rory remembered how Tally had reacted to her excuse of school work last time and abruptly redirected where the sentence had been going. She hadn't really known Tally all that well outside of the drunken parties they'd attended together and wondered now whether what she was facing in the other girl was something akin to abandonment issues. Had Tally decided Rory was a closer friend of hers than Rory had known or could remember?

"I—Sure, uh, I need to return these books. But then—"

"Didn't we have plans to—" Smithy started, speaking over her words.

But Tally was just as quick to ride over him, not even looking at him as she said, "Yeah, yeah, we can get to that later. We have to eat first!" She seemed so happy now that plans had been made to all have dinner together. Stepping further away from Smithy, Tally slipped her hand into the small spot at the crook of Rory arm around where she was holding her books.

Rory's jaw clenched, her eyes closed. She couldn't help but think of the way she and Michelle had linked arms the night before, and gritted her teeth against linking the two women together like that. She and Tally were on such different wavelengths. But Rory had no idea how to get that across to her in a way that she would listen to.

She could hear Smithy trying to say something

behind them, and vaguely hoped he would talk Tally out of following. Tally disregarded him again.

"So how are your classes going?" Tally asked, falling into step with her easily.

"They're good," Rory answered, summoning a smile to her lips. Since Tally was trying so hard, did that mean Rory was obliged to do the same? But surely if they were just going to eat dinner before Smithy and Tally went to some party, Rory wasn't in trouble. She tried to tell herself to relax, not overthink things. "They're actually really good. I like my 14th century England lecturer. She runs lectures like an extended tutorial. We have a lecture hall that's small enough, so it works."

"Oh, that sounds good. Hey, do you remember that essay Matthew handed in a week late? He still got an 87% on it, the bastard!"

Matthew was someone they used to get high with. Last time Rory had checked, he did a bit of dealing on the side.

He was *not* someone Rory felt comfortable discussing right now.

"Mmm," she answered, noncommittally. She wished she knew where Smithy stood on all this. From the way he'd tried to interject earlier, she might have thought he was attempting to give her an easy way out of… this. Whatever this was. It was another example of kindness that made Rory wish she hadn't met him as part of the party crowd.

Rory wracked her brain for someone or something else she and Tally could talk about, for some other thing they had in common except for alcohol and the people with whom they went to uni. Surely there had been other things they had in common. Or had every one of their conversations up till now been about blowing off steam after classes and drinking?

"I don't want to eat on campus," Tally said after Rory couldn't think of a single thing to say. "We do that everyday. There are other places to eat not too far from here. We could take a tram up High Street and see where it takes us."

As far as innocent conversation starters went, Rory couldn't fault it. But she didn't want to just take a wander up and down High Street either. There were far too many bars there and every restaurant she could think of other than Kismet sold alcohol.

"Ah, sorry, I can't," Rory said, before embellishing on the lie she'd started with. "My mum's picking me up from here after dinner. I'm staying at her place tonight. If we go off campus, it won't give us enough time to have dinner together." She deliberately inserted a wheedling tone into her voice, like it would disappoint her too much if they didn't have dinner together now after all this. It was manipulative and Rory wasn't proud of it, but it was also survival.

It worked. Tally's eyebrows shot right up, and she let go of her arm to again go into full body hugging Rory just like when they'd first come upon each other. "Aww, we'll definitely make time to have dinner together, don't you worry about it! We'll just eat off campus another night."

Reaching the library, Rory put her books down into the shoot, freeing herself from Tally to do it. She hated the way her heart raced every moment she was around the other girl now. She couldn't think straight. She felt like her only recourse was to react, constantly scared that she would be too slow, would miss something, would wake up to find herself in a drunken mess that she couldn't get out of.

But she couldn't really blame Tally for that either. It wasn't Tally's fault that Rory couldn't give in to even one drink without knowing she'd go off the rails completely. It was just that… She didn't feel that was something she could say without Tally using it against her. That story wasn't something she wanted to just give to Tally, who could then do anything at all with it that she wanted. Rory honestly didn't know Tally well enough to know that she wouldn't.

No. She just had to keep her balance in this dangerous game for as long as she was able.

She led Tally and Smithy to a table for four outside a café that served lunch and dinner for students opposite the library. The food was cheap and relatively harmless. Smithy watched the table for them as Tally dragged Rory up to the counter with her to order.

"Now how are you going, really?" There were three people in line in front of them. Rory tried to look preoccupied with deciding what she wanted to order, but they'd all been here to grab focaccias on the go and were relatively well acquainted with the short list of what was on the menu. "You know you can tell me."

Tally's eyes were wide and guileless as she looked up at Rory. Rory's lips parted. Tally looked so reasonable right then that Rory wondered whether it might not be a good idea to get what she was feeling out in the open after all. If Tally reacted poorly, Rory could judge her then, instead of before.

"I've been thinking, you know...?" Rory started, but it proved more difficult than she thought to push the words out.

"Mmm?" Tally murmured, raising her eyebrows and nodding her head encouragingly.

"Been thinking that, well, you know, we're in our third year of university this year."

A continued silent bobbing of the head was her only answer.

"Well, I kinda thought, it might be time, I mean... Everyone starts to grow up sometime, don't they? It's just, kinda inevitable."

"I *know*!" Tally said, surprising her. Rory smiled, relieved and thinking this was a good sign. "Raelene got herself pregnant. Did you hear? She says that Joel's the dad, but Joel says he never touched her."

Rory struggled to keep the smile stretched on her lips at this outpouring. All of a sudden, there was a whooshing in her ears and she struggled to hear the continued babbling of what amounted to a story between people she didn't care about. Had she even met Joel? Why would Raelene tell anyone that someone was the dad if it wasn't true? Had she even been sober when the kid had been conceived? She heard that having a child changed a person, but it would want to change Raelene a *lot* before she was someone Rory would be comfortable leaving a child around.

Tally's rambling story came to an end. "You know?" she prompted, when Rory didn't immediately say anything.

"Oh… yeah," Rory said, at a loss. Their conversation resembled nothing of the one about growing up and maybe not drinking so much that she'd intended to have. But at least they were at the front of the line and could stop talking for a while.

They each made their orders and took the number back to the table so that Smithy could stand and make his order, the line already longer than when they'd first gotten into it. Back at the table, Rory once again found that there was nothing to distract herself or Tally but each other.

Nothing except Rory's worry over the previous conversation. She tried again to remember what had happened before she woke up with Tally and that other guy in bed beside her.

"Tally..." Rory started. "That night of the last party I went to... Did we... you and me and that other guy... Did we... before we went to bed..."

Tally narrowed her eyes. It looked like she was trying to peer between the spaces and pauses in Rory's words to find some sense or understanding. Eventually, her eyes widened and she leaned back in her chair. She finally got it, Rory thought. At least, she hoped she'd finally got it.

"Oohhhh!" The sound was drawn out, with a tinkling laugh at the end. Rory gritted her teeth at each second she had to wait to find out if Tally really understood what she was trying to say this time, or was about to go off on her own tangent. "Yeaaaah, that was a good night, wasn't it? I thought we scared you off with that—"

"What happened?" Rory interjected, cutting her off sharply.

Tally looked surprised, maybe because it was the first time Rory had ever spoken to her like that.

"Please," Rory added, belatedly.

"Well... you know what happened, don't you?" Tally asked, but there was something childlike and hesitant in the lift of the words, as though she was waiting for the punch line that would make Rory's question make sense again.

Rory gave a very slight headshake.

"*No*," Tally said, pushing all the emphasis that had been absent in her last sentence into that one word. "You didn't tell me that!"

Rory shrugged.

"Is *that* why you've been acting so weird lately?"

Rory didn't say anything. Truthfully, if Tally decided to look back, she would notice that it had started before then, but Rory wasn't about to point that part out.

"Oh, hon." Tally laid a hand on top of Rory. Rory, so focused on the conversation they were finally having, didn't pull away. "We didn't *sleep* together, if that's what you mean."

That was exactly what she meant, but on its own it wasn't enough. "And… that other guy?"

"He was passed out on the bed when we found it. You figured there was enough space for both of us still. We rock-paper-scissored to see who would sleep in the middle."

So. That was that, then. It almost seemed as though she had made a big fuss out of nothing. Except, Rory knew she hadn't. There had still been that other guy, who had actually told her… told her.

Sitting right there, in front of Tally and Smithy, her mind had a flashback to it.

Rory woke up to someone on top of her, sucking face with her formerly unconscious body.

She yelled and pushed him off, even as the familiar pain of a hangover hit only a second later. While the unknown man fell onto the floor, Rory concentrated on not making any more sudden movements that might jar her head.

"What the hell?" came the voice from the floor.

Rory winced from behind closed eyes and pressed her hand against her forehead, more to keep her brain on the inside of her skull than anything else.

"Next time you try kissing a girl, maybe make sure she's awake," she said, not daring to take her eyes off him for a moment despite the pain.

"Oh, right, cause you weren't into it when we went to bed last night," came the biting reply.

Rory didn't know about that. Braving the promise of pain, pulled her hand away from her head. "We slept together last night?" she probed, squinting.

Matt snorted as he stood up. "I'll tell them how drunk you were if you try to trump up a rape charge. Everyone saw how you were last night."

"Rory?" Tally was looking at her, frowning slightly, and Rory realised she hadn't spoken for a while, hadn't replied to what Tally had said.

"Thanks, Tally." Only barely did Rory manage to keep from rubbing her hand against her brow and letting the tears fall. She could feel them, pressing against the backs of her eyelids. So far, Rory hadn't had any flashbacks to the sex she hadn't wanted or consented to having. She desperately hoped it stayed that way.

"Of course! Geez, if that's been what's been bothering you, you only had to ask!" Tally looked up as Smithy came back towards the table, having made his order. "We've finally figured out what's been making Rory act so weird, and we're all made up again. Isn't that great? This calls for a round of drinks!"

Tally missed it, because she was facing Smithy, but Rory whole face blanched. And yet, at the same time, it was the perfect way to escape the memories that talking with Tally had brought back up again.

Tally's face swung around to her again. "You in?" she demanded.

Rory offered a smile because the other option was to cry. "You know I am."

Chapter Six

It was 9.30 p.m. when Smithy had prompted, not for the first time, that Rory was supposed to go to her mum's that night. The first time he said it, Rory had pulled out her phone and pretended to send a text to her mum. The second time he said it, Rory and Tally were in the middle of this amazing conversation that Rory didn't want to stop, and she didn't quite register that a text message from Michelle was sitting on her screen.

The third time Smithy mentioned it, Rory was halfway through her third glass of cider. She and Tally were in the middle of catching their breath from almost hysterical laughter. Something about the small pile of clear, empty glasses that she and Tally had managed to amass—Smithy had had the first round with them, then abstained—struck an off chord in her. It might have been an attempt at solidarity, but Rory had missed it completely. The half empty pint of cider sat directly in front of her, its messy condensation creating a fallen ring around it on the table. Laughter didn't bubble up in the back of her throat, but a broken sob did.

Rory did her best to swallow it, her wide-eyed gaze stretching itself to Smithy and finding somewhere it could ground itself there.

"Yes." She took her phone from the table, where it was sitting next to the sweating cider that still urged her to drink it. "Shit," she said, entirely unfeigned as she saw Michelle's text message again. "I didn't realise the time."

"Go." Tally waved her off with a laugh. "I'll drink the rest of this."

There was a spark of a moment where Rory's thoughts jealously guarded the rest of her cider, but she stumbled out of her chair and took a large step back before her physical actions could echo the thought.

"Oops, careful!" Tally said. The laughter that rang in her voice was the same that had debilitated them both only a moment before.

Rory gulped in a breath of air, trying for the fresh night air untainted by the smell of fermented fruit.

"Hey, why don't you let me walk you home?" Smithy asked, looking concerned.

Tally slapped him lightly on the arm as she snorted. "She lives ten streets away from campus. It's not like she's hiking into the desert."

"I'll be fine on my own," Rory said in a quiet voice that only she and Smithy noticed.

He nodded once, seemed about to say something more, then nodded again. Rory firmed her lips, and swung her body away from the table, and the empty glasses, without another word.

She didn't need a pretence that her mum was picking her up, for all Tally cared about it, she thought bitterly. She felt wetness on her cheeks long before she actually recognised she was crying.

Her place promised her questions she didn't want to answer if Helene was home. She couldn't go back to the library without chancing that she'd walk by Tally and Smithy. Instead, she walked to the tree where Michelle had kissed her for the first time. Leaning against its reassuring trunk, and feeling safe in the comfort of darkness plus branches that would obscure the view of anyone looking towards her, Rory pulled out her phone. She had to wait several moments for the tears to clear enough to see the screen after the alert that told her it was an hour and 34 minutes since the message had been received.

I know you are probably out doing fun university things, but I wanted to say I miss you and I'm thinking of you.

Rory gave a little sob under her breath. *I miss you too*, she texted longingly.

I'm flattered! Busy day?

not so busy. not such fun with university things either, Rory texted back.

I am sorry to hear that.

Several more tears slipped down Rory cheeks, as she slipped the phone into the back pocket of her jeans. She didn't deserve nice words. She didn't deserve Michelle's sweetness. Even knowing what she was doing, Rory couldn't make herself stop. Tally hadn't poured cider down her throat; Rory had done that on her own. Three times!

She couldn't bring herself to text Michelle anymore that night because she didn't feel she deserved to. She didn't deserve nice trees or sweet memories of kisses. She deserved someone telling her off. She wanted some sort of punishment, for the internal chastisements in her head to become external.

Rory closed her eyes and leaned her head back against the harsh bark of the tree trunk. Michelle didn't even know. She couldn't bear to think how fast Michelle would run if she knew how much trouble Rory was. Nobody would want to be near her. Rory didn't even want to be near herself. Not that that she was given a choice.

After her self-banishment from the tree, the library, and her own home, there was only one more place to go. Kismet was open 'til eleven on Thursday and Friday nights. It was after the dinner rush and there were some tables free. Rory slipped gratefully into a chair beside a wall mural depicting *Where the Wild Things Are*. Shortly thereafter, a woman around Michelle's age in a red apron and with a nametag reading 'Steve' came around with a cup and a bottle of water.

"You expecting anyone else tonight?"

Rory shook her head. "No," she said on an exhale, then covered her mouth behind her hand as the woman walked away. They didn't sell alcohol here. If she reeked of cider, would they assume what had brought her here? Another part of the low-income group who came in here included the down on their luck crowd. Rory almost sunk down onto the table in embarrassment. She had never thought she would be one of those people at Kismet.

The thought was so devastating, it brought tears to her eyes and bile to her throat. For several moments, she just couldn't think past it. In desperation, Rory cast her gaze towards the table where she'd first seen Michelle. But there was no one sitting there.

"Has someone taken your order?"

Another waiter had come by. Rory looked at him, then tilted her head away as she spoke. "No. I was just heading off."

There was no comfort for her here. She'd only really come out because she felt like she couldn't go home. But if Helena wanted to ask her questions about why she was crying or anything else, Rory had just as much right not to answer, she supposed.

The tram ride back down High Street was quiet. There were almost no other passengers, despite the fact that the trams only came by every half hour at this time of night. Rory zoned out to the point where she almost missed her stop twenty minutes down the road.

It was just under a ten-minute walk from the tram stop to her place and she walked every pace of it with heavy feet. Her phone display said it just before 10:30 p.m. when she pushed open the door. When the lack of lights and movement in the room struck her, Rory almost didn't know what to do. For a moment, she stood dumb in the doorway, an arc of light from the hall flooding into the room. The soft snoring of Helena's in and outward breath was a further testament to Helena's state of rest. Rory shut the door quietly.

In darkness, she navigated her way across the living room towards her bedroom. Once there, she attempted to breathe, to just regulate her breathing so she didn't feel it was about to strangle her.

After that, she lay down on top of the blankets at first. Then, she got up, got changed, slipped out of the room to pad down and brush her teeth in the bathroom, and into the bed. She would sleep this off. It wouldn't feel so bad the morning after. She'd already washed the taste and smell of alcohol from her breath, and even if she burped it would be a strange combined taste of apples and mint. Rory thought she could deal with that.

For forty five minutes, she told herself she could do exactly that, as she tossed and turned in her bed, waiting for the thoughts to abate and sleep to take her.

When that didn't happen, and Rory couldn't stand another rotation on her back, front, side and back again, staring at the ceiling, she picked up the phone and dialled Michelle.

Michelle answered on the second ring.

"I wasn't expecting a call." But it was a pleasant surprise; Rory could hear the smile in her voice.

"Did I wake you?" she whispered.

"Not even remotely," Michelle reassured her. "But why are you whispering?"

"Housemate sleeping," Rory answered.

"Ah." Michelle paused for a while, but when Rory didn't say anything, she murmured, "So what caused you to ring, sweetheart?"

"Just wanted to hear your voice." Rory closed her eyes and pushed half of her face hard into the pillow. It was wet, she realised, across the cheekbone and over the brow. She wasn't strong. She wasn't strong enough.

"Would you like me to come around?"

"No, I don't need you to do that."

Michelle made a sound that was like a soft growl, or a purring laugh. "I don't need to…"

"You have work early in the morning." Weakening, weakening.

"And?"

"Okay."

"Okay, you want me to come around?"

"Yes."

A pause. Then, "Are you okay, sweetheart?"

Rory shook her head. Then she remembered that Michelle couldn't see her but chose to remain silent anyway.

A moment later, Michelle hummed down the line. "Hmm. I'll be there in about twenty minutes."

Rory hung up. She wasn't crying, but only just.

All her attention was focused on that. She hadn't noticed when Helena's snoring had stopped midway through the call.

Helena reached up to turn on her bedside lamp as Rory stepped out into the hall between their rooms. The sudden light caught Rory's eyes. "I'm sorry," she said, not quite able to face her housemate in case there were still signs of her recent crying. She hadn't yet glanced at the bathroom mirror to see how bad the damage was. "I didn't mean to wake you."

"I didn't realise it was a girl," Helena said. "That you were dating, I mean. I thought you were interested in guys."

"I am," Rory said vaguely waving a hand vaguely. She really didn't need a conversation about her bisexuality on top of everything else tonight.

The word 'bisexual' seemed to hover on the air between them nonetheless. Again, Rory mind flashed to the drunken nights kissing Tally. It was different with Michelle. Rory tried to replay the conversation she'd just had with Michelle in her head, to figure out how much Helena might have overheard. She realised, then, it didn't matter.

"Oh." Helena didn't say anything for a long enough time after that that Rory made her escape into the bathroom, turned on the light and closed the door.

Twenty minutes, Michelle had said. How much time had passed since then? Rory tried to straighten herself out, gargled some Listerine and hoped the smell of cider wasn't seeping from her pores.

She hadn't been in the bathroom more than ten minutes by the time she came back out again, but Helena's light was still on.

"Try to get back to sleep," she whispered to her.

"Where are you going?" Helena asked curiously.

"My girlfriend's coming to pick me up," Rory answered simply.

~~*

Rory waited in the usual spot on the nature strip. She had on a loose fitting jacket because the late night had brought with it a cool wind and recognised Michelle's car when it pulled up to the place where she'd parked the last time.

"What are you doing waiting out here?" Michelle asked as Rory got into her car. "It's too cold. I was just going to call you."

Rory shrugged. Michelle looked at her with concern and then slowly pulled away from the curb.

Unlike with Helena, Rory didn't feel the need to share, to fill in the silence with useless words that were just as likely to make the situation worse. She felt comfortable with Michelle, even if Michelle didn't know what was going on inside

Rory's head.

They pulled in at a parking lot near a train station, and Rory looked up at Michelle with surprise.

"I thought: late night pancakes," Michelle said, her voice betraying some sense of pride.

"Do you know all the cool, random places to eat out here?" Rory asked.

"Most of them," Michelle answered with satisfaction. "Come on."

Rory smiled. She couldn't help it. Half an hour ago, she'd felt almost like she'd never smile again, but here Michelle was, drawing it out of her like it was easy.

"Thank you," Rory said, and both of them knew that she was thanking Michelle for more than late night pancakes.

"You're very welcome." Michelle leaned over the handbrake between them and Rory leaned into the kiss. "I hadn't said a proper hello yet," she murmured, as she pulled away.

"I get that," Rory said, feeling warm and fuzzy in a way that had nothing to do with alcohol.

They lingered together in the car a little longer before Michelle opened the car door and cool night air pushed its way into the warmth of the car. Michelle had her fingers entwined with Rory as soon as they walked around the car and were striding side by side. It wasn't a long walk to late night pancakes. Michelle opened the door for Rory.

"Okay, opening doors, paying for our meals?" Rory said, once they'd found a table together and sat down. "I don't think of chivalry as something a woman usually does."

"Why should chivalry be gendered at all?" Michelle asked.

It was a good point, and one to which Rory didn't have an answer.

Michelle looked up towards the menu that was written in chalk above the kitchen area, and Rory followed her gaze. There were sweet and savoury pancakes, as well as a selection of hot and iced drinks. This time, rather than ordering to share, they ordered a sweet pancake each.

The pancakes were more like crêpes, wrapped around chopped fruit and sugar or maple syrup. Rory's even had goat cheese that was oozing against the open end of the roll.

They ended up sharing again, each of them eating half of their own pancakes, before pushing their plates across the table and the second half of the other's.

"That was amazing," Rory said. "And now I'm seriously stuffed."

She leaned back against her chair, but reached her hand out across the table when Michelle reached hers out to hold it. They still each had half of the hot chocolates they had ordered first, but ignored them in favour of staring at each other instead.

"At the risk of saying it too early in the

relationship," Michelle murmured, her adoring expression not changing at all with the words. "I'm worried about you."

Rory shifted, and would have pulled her hand away from Michelle's if the other girl hadn't tightened her grip.

"I understand if you don't want to talk about it yet," Michelle continued, now that she obviously had Rory's full attention. "We haven't known each other very long, and it's your choice. But I do care. I'm right here. And I'm glad you called me tonight."

She loosened her grasp again. Rory hesitated a moment, considering whether to pull her hand away now that she could. But she didn't. That in itself seemed to send its own message to Michelle. She smiled, that quirky, slightly knowing grin.

"I'm not ready to talk about it," Rory said. It was clear that it was her move, and this time the silence between them did compel her to talk, even if it was to say that she wasn't ready to talk. "Yet."

Michelle nodded her head. "As I said: it is your choice." The knowing smirk was still there, both on her lips and in her eyes, softening what might otherwise have sounded like censure.

"Thank you," Rory said again. But she didn't know why this time. In an attempt to unpack it, she said, "For not being pushy, for understanding. For letting me know that you… that you…"

"Care?" Michelle finished for her.

Rory nodded mutely.

"I think we've covered that." Michelle's eyes were sharp behind the glasses. Rory had a growing understanding that she didn't miss much. The cheeky grin that lifted the corners of her lips filled Rory with the urge to kiss that mouth again.

It was an urge, finally, that she could give into without guilt.

She got up and, under Michelle's watchful eye, moved around the table until they were sitting on the same side. For twenty minutes, the two girls spent their time with kissing and tasteful in public petting.

Eventually, though, it came to the time when their plates had been taken away and their hot chocolates were cold. It was midnight.

"I should get you home, dear one," Michelle said softly.

"I... don't want to go home."

Michelle seemed indulgent, but calculating at the same time. "I can't be up all night. Fridays are our busiest days, just before the weekend."

Rory flushed. "I wasn't... I didn't..."

Amusement had wiped the indulgence from her face, but there was still something calculating there behind her eyes, something she was wondering about, but wasn't saying. "Calm down, pet. I was only teasing."

Rory tried to see the amusement in it, too, she really did. But all she could think about was that she didn't really have an option but to go back to her place tonight. Her mum's house was really too far to ask Michelle to take her, and public transport was no longer running.

"Can you find a way to wherever you need to go from my place tomorrow?" Michelle asked. "After I go to work? You said there was a tram last time."

Rory shook her head, not wanting to impose. "I didn't mean to expect…!"

Michelle waved off her concern. "We're dating. It's completely fine for you to come back to my place. Besides, it'll be nice to have someone else to cuddle with in bed for a change."

Her eyelashes fluttered down, covering her eyes for just a moment so that Rory couldn't be certain it was sadness she'd seen for a second there. She couldn't deny Michelle's words, though. Having someone else in the bed—someone she remembered getting into the bed with—would be nice for her too.

A moment passed, then two, and then Michelle stood up. Like last time, she extended her hand down to Rory, waiting for her to take it. "Come now. Let's head back to mine."

~~*

She'd been here before, but this time it was different. Last time, she hadn't had more than a glance over Michelle's bedroom on their way out to somewhere else. This time, she was sleeping here.

Michelle directed them both straight into that room, rather than stopping by to turn on any of the lights in the lounge room. A spare nightie was put out on the bed, and Rory was encouraged into the en suite to get changed into it for sleeping.

She got changed quickly, throwing off her own clothing in a pile on the floor tiles and pulling on the nightie without letting herself think about it too much. She then hesitated in the bathroom, aware that Michelle may have taken her own time, and not wanting to walk in on her half undressed. Not after Michelle had explicitly stated that she needed to go straight to sleep tonight.

The lamps on the bedside tables either side of Michelle's bed were on when Rory walked out of the bathroom. A dim orange light lit the room. Michelle was pulling up the covers on her side of the bed, near the closed-curtain window on the other side of the room. Rory closed the bathroom door behind her and followed suit, pulling up the covers and slipping underneath, reaching up to turn the lamp on her side off.

The room dimmed even further.

"Come here," Michelle murmured. She'd taken her glasses off already. There was still enough light that Rory could see the glint of Michelle's eyes, her bare shoulders above the covers, her black hair splayed across the white pillow behind her. One of her arms lifted the covers between them, offering invitingly a space much closer for Rory to lie.

Rory scooted across the clean sheets and into Michelle's arms. Michelle turned away from her for only a moment, reaching up to turn off her lamp in turn. That was the last time Michelle turned away from her through the night.

In utter blackness—the curtains didn't let in even the light from outside street lights, much better quality than the ones in her cheap unit—Rory could only feel the soft mattress beneath her, the steady breathing of Michelle behind her, and the warm weight of Michelle's arms around her. The rest of the house was silent, given that Michelle lived alone. There was no sound of other person's snoring or shifting around on a bed in the next room.

Still, even with all that comfort, Rory lay awake and unable to sleep. It was too different, too obviously not her own room. The fact that Michelle had fallen asleep so easily only made it worse. Rory's right arm fell asleep under her, but she felt like she couldn't move in case she woke Michelle up. So she just lay there, waiting to find out if there was another sensation to come after the numbness.

Eventually, she fell asleep. She knew that because she woke up again when Michelle's alarm went off.

"Wha' time's it?" she mumbled, her face still pressed against the pillow. The light was only just starting to come around the windows. Just because she was awake, didn't mean she was ready to move yet.

Michelle kissed her temple and pushed herself up from the bed, which dipped and caused Rory to roll ever so slightly backwards towards the other girl.

"It's 6:30," Michelle said. "Don't feel like you have to get up. The door locks easily from the inside, and you can message me if you have any trouble when you're leaving."

"Kay," Rory murmured. Despite not moving, she did open her eyes as Michelle rounded the bed towards the bathroom. The other girl was gorgeous in a form fitting black satin nightgown. For once, her black hair was rumpled, though Rory found that look even more alluring. She might even have said something to that effect if Michelle hadn't disappeared into the bathroom.

The shower started a moment later, and Rory closed her eyes again. She missed it when Michelle came out of the bathroom, missed her moving around the room and getting dressed into her work gear. The next she knew, Michelle's thumb grazed her cheekbone and her lips pressed lightly against Rory's a moment later.

"See you soon, pet," Michelle murmured.

Rory found she really liked that endearment. Moments later, she heard the front door close.

Chapter Seven

Rory started the morning by helping herself to a couple of pieces of toast and some coffee in Michelle's kitchen. She didn't have any classes on a Friday morning, so there was no point in hurrying. She wandered into the bathroom for a nice long shower, in the process missing a phone call from her mum, which she once again didn't return.

She ended up back in Michelle's room, cross-legged in the middle of the bed, considering posting something online from her phone.

Something weird is happening to me, she started. *I'm sitting in the bedroom of a girl that I've been seeing. Someone who's incredibly sweet. Listens to me when I've got things to say. Lets me stay silent when I don't want to talk. It started at the beginning of semester…*

The only people who were left on her social media after the friends cull were largely family and friends from high school and, of course, Helena. Rory wasn't sure how her housemate would deal with this post after the way she reacted the night before. She didn't know how any of the people still on her list would respond to it. Rory scrolled up with her thumb, trying to read

One Last Drop

this post the way that any of them might. Trying to figure out how she could end it without saying too much.

None of them would understand, she realised. Although she'd spoken to her mum a couple of years ago about identifying as bisexual, none of her extended family knew, and she wasn't sure that was the message she wanted high school friends she didn't often talk to anymore to read it.

Rory deleted the last few sentences she'd written, but before she knew it, she deleted it all. The memory of those feelings stayed with her, though, making her smile as her toes wriggled in Michelle's blankets.

Finally, Rory hopped on a bus that took her close enough to her place that she could walk the rest of the way.

Locked the door behind me, no troubles, Rory texted to Michelle.

A little after three p.m., Helena came back from uni. She stopped when she saw Rory sitting cross-legged on the couch.

"Hey," she said, and Rory replied in kind.

For a while, it looked like Helena wasn't going to say anything else. Then, she said, "I don't know how you get away with it."

"I'm sorry, what?" Rory blinked. She had spent so much time focused on her drinking troubles that it hadn't occurred to her until then that she could be seen as 'getting away' with something by dating another woman.

Helena's eyes widened. "I don't mean to offend you. I'd just be worried about what other people would say. I'd be too scared to do it."

"Well, it's probably not something you'd want to do, if that's all that's what would stop you," Rory offered with a smile to try to offset too much harshness.

But maybe she should have been harsh in her reply to Helena. She knew Helena well enough to know she didn't mean anything by it, but who really cared about the gender of the person she decided to date? It was 2017 already. Whose business was it of anyone other than hers and Michelle's?

Helena seemed about to say something more when Rory's phone went off. Turning her back to Helena, Rory pulled out her phone and read the text that'd just come through.

How would you feel about going to a house party with me and some friends of mine tonight? Michelle asked.

Rory didn't need to think before replying. *i would feel really good about that. What time?*

~~*

Rory chose her clothes to match with the kinds Michelle usually wore. Rory all but lived in her jeans, but she didn't think she'd ever seen Michelle in a pair. Black pants didn't seem quite right, too formal, but she didn't have any skirts. In the end,

Rory went for a pair of black pinstriped jeans that were all but new and all the way at the back of her chest of drawers. For a top, she grabbed an army green baby doll tee and looped a grey scarf around her neck, pulling it down as far as her sternum.

When she arrived at Michelle's door and was let in, Michelle was in a floor length black skirt, bare feet and a deep blue lace top with loose sleeves.

"You're early," she said, giving Rory a kiss before closing the door.

Rory smirked. "I think you've lost track of time," she answered.

That made Michelle's eyes widen before she turned and shot into her bedroom. "Shit!" she said. Rory wisely made the decision to stay standing by the door. "I'll only be a second longer."

"Maybe grab some shoes?" Rory said cheekily.

"Maybe." Michelle growled her reply.

When she came out of her room the second time, her hair was slightly curled at the ends, she wore shoes and had a small, black bag over one shoulder.

"Okay," she said, in what was about as close as Rory had ever seen her look to 'sheepish'.

Rory diplomatically refrained from commenting on it.

The drive wasn't so far from Michelle's house. The MP3 player in Michelle's car was playing an industrial sounding track. The air conditioner was on low, enough to set a breeze through the car, but not enough to blow their hair around.

"Do your friends know much about me?" Rory asked.

"I may have mentioned you."

Rory turned her head to glance at Michelle. Her painted lips were slightly curved as though something was amusing to her. Rory was starting to know Michelle well enough to know that that particular smirk was usually at her expense.

When they got out of the car, the gentle evening wind gave Michelle's locks a windswept look on the walk between car and house. Rory frowned, trying desperately to straighten her own hair into some semblance of order. She was still in the middle of it when the door opened and the house's occupant took Michelle into an affectionate hug.

"You must be Rory. I'm Gemma."

Rory found through the hug she received that the party was full of particularly touchy people.

"What can I get you guys to drink?" Gemma asked them as they walked towards the kitchen. Rory had prepared herself for the question this time, ever since Michelle had mentioned the words 'house party'.

"Do you have cola?" she asked.

"Definitely. It's in the fridge. Help yourself."

Michelle asked for a cranberry and vodka, which Gemma made for her while Rory poured her cola, almost full to the brim so she could nurse it without anyone asking if she wanted another drink. Michelle then took her into the lounge room so she could introduce her to the rest of her friends.

"This is Tim," she said, pointing to a neat looking brunette in a short-sleeved, button up shirt. He lifted a hand for a two-fingered wave from where he was lounging on the floor, his back against the couch between two women introduced as Steve and Katrina.

"Make yourselves at home," Gemma said, floating her arm in a gesture that was already half forgotten as she turned towards another knock at the front door.

The energy of the room was high with so many talking and greeting each other at once, multiple conversations starting and then continuing. There were some, like Tim, who were content to sit and hold court as others like Gemma could be seen zipping between kitchen, hall and living room, the ghost of her skirt swishing around corners as she went between conversations.

Rory took another sip of her drink, content to sit next to Katrina, with Michelle perched on the couch arm beside her.

Michelle was in her element. She had kicked off her heels almost as soon as she entered the house. It seemed the heels had been included in Michelle's outfit tonight solely for the sake of a previous conversation—half finished and before Rory time—between her and Steve. The two women seemed to have the monopoly on sitting on the edge of the cushion, stiff spined, despite the comfy lounge quality of the couches. They looked at each other and spoke over the heads of the three individuals between them. Tim seemed inured to the situation; Katrina amused. Taking her cue from the others, Rory dipped her head, bemused, to drink more cola.

Gemma came back to them in a flurry. Her face was flushed, lips swollen and she smiled. Rory wondered what was going on in the other room.

"I've been a dreadful host," she said, squatting down on the carpet in front of Rory.

"Dreadful," Tim agreed drolly.

Gemma swatted him, which he made no effort to avoid. "I haven't got to know you at all!" she said, her attention returning to Rory.

"Oh." Rory blinked. "What did you want to know?"

"Well, Michelle told us you were at uni. What are you studying?" Gemma shuffled on the balls of her feet, attempting to find a more comfortable position.

"European feudalism," Rory answered. Then, "Sociology," she added.

"Oh, I have a friend who did gender studies," Gemma said, nodding.

Rory was not unused to this interpretation. So she nodded, her mouth stretching into a thin-lipped smile while she tried to think of something constructive to add beyond how separate the studies of gender and feudalism were.

She took too long. Gemma stood up abruptly, winced, and shifted from foot to foot as feeling seemed to return to them. Still waving her right foot about, she told Rory, "I'm getting you a drink. What would you like?"

Rory lifted her cup of cola, the same one from the start of the night. "I'm still good."

"You've had that for more than an hour and a half. I'm surprised it isn't flat by now." Gemma wasn't drunk, although she'd obviously had one or two drinks. Her cheeks were flushed and her comment showed more about what she thought made up a good hostess than anything else. She made for the kitchen on comfortably bare feet, glancing over her shoulder once. "Scotch and Coke, wasn't it?" she asked.

Rory opened her mouth to correct that it was just cola, but that wasn't what came out of her mouth.

"Yes. Thank you." Pushing up off the floor, Rory followed the shorter girl, bringing her cup with her.

Gemma unceremoniously poured the remains of the cup down the sink. "It's great that you came tonight. Michelle really likes you."

"Really?" Rory cast a glance across the kitchen bench to where Michelle was sitting. She'd delicately changed her position from couch arm to couch cushion, her body tilted towards Steve, but her gaze met Rory across the room. Rory caught her breath. Foolish to do so. She already knew Michelle liked her. They were dating. But, there was dating, and there was *dating*. And there was still so much that Michelle didn't know about her.

She couldn't help but worry that Michelle's feelings would change once she really did get to know her.

Her shoulders tense, Rory's hands clung to the kitchen bench. Looking down at the white patches over her knuckles, she deliberately let go of the kitchen bench. She gratefully held onto the newly filled cup Gemma was holding out to her. She didn't quite dare to look over to the couch and see if Michelle was still looking in her direction or had gone back to her own conversation.

"What's Michelle said?" Rory asked instead, lifting the cup up to her lips. The bitterness of scotch seared her mouth and jumped to the back of her throat even as the sweetness of cola filled her mouth. Rory felt alive for the first time that night. The world snapped into a sharper focus.

"Oh, you know," Gemma said, pouring a drink for herself. "She feels like she can be herself around you, blah blah blah." She turned away from the drink, while still pouring, in order to roll her eyes at Rory in the self-deprecating way of someone describing affection. She shook her head at herself, before turning back to the glass only just before it overflowed. "Oops!" Very carefully, she set it down on the bench, but not before some swished onto her thumb.

"We're a bit protective of Michelle." Gemma lowered her voice. This told Rory that, although there was music in the background, and multiple conversations, this was a conversation she didn't want to chance Michelle overhearing. Gemma turned her back to the bench and leaned against it, licking the alcohol off her thumb absently. "She was hurt by her last girlfriend. Everyone's got baggage, right? But you seem really nice!"

Oh, Rory thought. If only they knew.

Chapter Eight

Rory finished the last mouthful of her scotch and Coke in a long swig. In the absence of anywhere else to put the glass, Rory kept it in her hand as she wandered with Gemma to the other room of the party. Katrina, from the first introductions, was the only person she knew there apart from Gemma.

Gemma jumped into the middle of two boys, skilfully managing not to spill the drink she held on either of them. They stopped the conversation they'd been engaging in with some girl with frosted fingernails.

"Having a good time there, are you?" one of them asked, as the other delicately plucked the cup from her hand and placed it on the side table.

"Hey, I was drinking that!" Gemma pouted.

"Not until you've stopped squirming," he told her.

Gemma frowned, but did as she was told, adjusting herself until she was sitting upright on top of them, her back against their shoulders. "Better?" she demanded, before her gaze set upon the forgotten Rory again. "Oh!" She absently accepted the cup that was brought back to her hands, using it to gesture towards Rory. "Have you guys met Rory yet? This is Brian and Tobey."

Unsure of which one of the boys was which, Rory gave an overly friendly wave. The smile that accompanied it came easier than it would have at the beginning of the night.

"Nice to meet you," Brian/Tobey said to her. He had a nice smile, which he offered to her complete with dimples, before returning his gaze back to Gemma indulgently and kissing her nose, which immediately scrunched up.

"You're Michelle's new girl?" the other boy said.

"It's pretty much my new nickname," Rory said archly.

"Ouch. Bad first impression," he said, rubbing the back of his neck with his free hand. "Nice to meet you, anyhow. Rory, wasn't it?"

"Yeah." She relaxed her arch expression, which seemed to put the other boy back at his ease. Which made it easier, when it came to her to ask, "I'm sorry, your name was…?"

"Brian." He had a nicer set of teeth than Tobey had, but fewer dimples. Gemma chose that moment to turn from Tobey to kiss Brian on the side of the neck, and Rory realised she had no idea the nature of this relationship in front of her. Although, she thought lightly, it did give a reason for Gemma's swollen lips from before.

"As we were saying," Steve started. She opened into something to do with the mechanics of a new computer software system… or something. Rory didn't really follow it. Her hand lifted her glass to her mouth, disappointed to remember it was already empty.

"I'm with you," Katrina said, appearing at her side and looping an arm through hers. "This conversation doesn't interest me either. Let's get some drinks."

In full agreement, Rory fell into step with Katrina. Words came easier to her now that she'd had a real drink. She replied to Katrina almost without thinking. "If the conversation didn't interest you, what were you still doing there?"

"Vague hope?" Katrina answered with an easy laugh. "Foolish hope," she amended, pretending embarrassment.

They were both laughing as they re-entered the kitchen. Katrina dove into the fridge, swinging her hips in time to the music that was playing background to the living room conversations. Rory spun in a small circle before upending the bottle of scotch she found on the counter into her glass, then Katrina's as she shoved her cup against Rory with a dull clink.

"I feel I've hardly seen you at all tonight," Michelle said. Her arm went around Rory waist from behind and she leaned in to kiss the side of Rory's neck.

"You have really great friends." Rory turned so she could kiss Michelle full on the mouth. The girl's mouth tasted of strawberry daiquiri liquor. Rory wondered if there was any more of it, and whether it was something someone would be willing to share with her after Rory had finished this next drink.

"Mm." Michelle's lips curved at the edges before they pulled apart, so that Rory could feel the movement against her lips. Her hand snaked out towards the scotch that Katrina had helpfully topped up with cola before going elsewhere and giving the two girls some space.

"Please, help yourself," Rory said with a small eye roll.

Michelle didn't. She instead slid it slowly across the kitchen counter until it was behind her. Outside of Rory's reach.

"Hey…" Rory said, confusion puckering the skin between her eyebrows.

"Hey," Michelle said in reply. Her face was a calm mask, but the eyes in that face were still sharp, even after a couple of drinks.

Rory breath hitched, but she held her ground.

"I don't think that's a good idea," Michelle said. She pitched her voice low, so that Rory almost had to strain to hear it. But at least nobody else overheard her. Rory also heard what Michelle wasn't saying. What neither of them were explicitly saying.

Rory broke eye contact first before those unspoken words became voiced.

"You're probably right." She tried to aim for a light tone of voice, trying to further lessen the intensity of the moment with an uncaring shrug, even as her gaze strayed to the glass behind Michelle; thought of the strawberry daiquiri taste of Michelle's mouth.

When Rory next dared look into Michelle's eyes, the severity of her observing gaze had shifted into something more indulgent. Michelle's gaze shifted up towards her hairline where, a moment later, her hand followed the passage of her glance. Rory closed her eyes and leaned into that caress, willing to let herself believe, just that minute, that everything was fine.

~~*

It wasn't fine. It was, in fact, very difficult to sit in the middle of a party where everyone was drinking—with the taste of scotch at the back of her throat—and not be able to properly imbibe. Especially with the taste of the scotch still in the back of her mouth. Maybe this was her punishment. She couldn't behave like an adult like all these other people, so she had to miss out completely. Rory also didn't want to embarrass Michelle in front of so many of her friends. She was torn between self-loathing and craving for the next drink.

Both Gemma and Katrina came around to make sure Rory was all right for drinks. They were very good at making sure she felt welcome in this new group of people, but it was so hard to answer.

For strength—whether Michelle meant for it or not—her fingers danced across Rory shoulder leaving prickles of sensation wherever she touched and helping her to withstand the craving for the alcohol by giving her something else to focus on. It was subtle, so so subtle, these little things Michelle did. Rory was never quite sure if she was seeing or imagining them.

She knew Michelle had had more than her to drink, and she'd been worried she'd see a worse side to Michelle. Strangely, though, it just made Michelle more charismatic, more witty and, if anything, more affectionate.

"Give me your hand, sweetheart."

Rory wasn't sure how long she'd been passively sitting in on the conversation happening around her. Katrina and Gemma were still bantering back and forth as fast as any sitcom, while Brian's head fell deeper and deeper into his hands as they alternately ganged up on him and mocked him.

It was nothing to give Michelle her hand. They held hands all the time. Right now, there was even space on the couch beside Michelle, so she wasn't even sitting in front of her on the floor. Extending her hand out to Michelle was simple.

Michelle held Rory hand palm up, so that the paler underside of Rory's arm was visible. As she began to use her other hand to stroke up and down the length of Rory's forearm, Rory relaxed into the sensation. As Michelle's fingernails increased the pressure, Rory felt a slight thrill run through her. It didn't take so much to imagine that Michelle held her in place, her hand on hers, and that the other one was her punishment. By the time Michelle's strokes were alternating in pressure from the sensuous pleasure of the light touch to something leaving light, red marks on the skin, Rory was thrumming.

Michelle kept her eyes on Rory at each change in intensity, reading the expressions crossing Rory's face and seeming pleased by what she saw there. When Katrina cackled loudly at something Gemma or Brian must have said, Rory was surprised to remember there were people outside of the two of them; that there were still people who were drinking at this party.

A short time after, Michelle lifted her nails from Rory's arm. Rory immediately pined at the sudden loss of sensation; tried to keep the feeling from her face. The knowing smirk on Michelle's face told Rory that she hadn't managed it.

"I've got to go the bathroom," Michelle murmured, hardly moving her lips as she gazed between Rory eyes and mouth. "Will you be all right on your own?"

Rory willingly fooled herself into thinking that Michelle was talking about being all right in a roomful of strangers. "I will," she said.

Michelle nodded once, then pushed up from the couch.

The chair was only spare for a moment before

Brian plomped down next to her.

"Got tired of getting picked on?" Rory guessed.

"Not that it's going to make a difference me sitting here," Brian said, with a roll of his eyes. "I hope Michelle treats you better than that," he said, loud enough to make Gemma turn her head and stick her tongue out at him.

"She treats me well," Rory said.

"And you treat her well," Brian said, with mock severity.

"Of course," Rory said, with just as much mock sageness.

"Good then, because we're—"

"Protective of Michelle." Rory nodded slowly, noting that this was the second time it had come up tonight. "So I've heard."

"Ah." Brian seemed chagrined. "I've gone and stepped in it again, haven't I?"

"Not at all," Rory said. "I mean, well, of course, you're all protective of her. She's your friend…"

"But you've heard it already tonight," Brian said.

"Pretty much."

"Has she…?" Brian peered at her as though unsure what next to say lest in he step in it a third time for the night. "Do you know…?"

Rory kindly decided to put him out of his misery. "I just know it has something to do with her ex. I haven't really pried."

"Ah." Brian's lips thinned but he nodded.

She might have asked him to elaborate on this

mysterious ex, despite not wanting to pry, except that Brian's gaze lifted from hers towards someone behind her.

"I like her." Brian put an arm around her shoulders as she started to turn so that she almost fell into him. Rory tried to make it look graceful. She didn't pull away. He was nice, Rory felt comfortable with this amount of closeness between them, even though she'd only met him tonight. Michelle just looked at Brian blandly.

"So do I," she murmured. Her gaze warmed as it moved from him to Rory. Rory's face heated. For some reason, although it wasn't anything Rory didn't already know, the acknowledgement given in front of Michelle's friend caused her to lower her gaze to the floor.

She didn't see the way that Michelle smiled.

"Do you mind if I have my seat back?" Michelle asked of Brian. Rory wasn't sure if it was the alcohol or the question that had Michelle's voice purring like that. The husky sound of it put a shiver down Rory's back even before Brian vacated the seat and Michelle re-joined her.

The first touch of Michelle's hand on her forearm was electric. Rory looked down at it as if vaguely surprised it was still attached to her when she realised she hadn't moved her hand or arm since Michelle had gone.

When she looked back up into Michelle's eyes, there was a slight raise of the girl's eyebrow waiting for her. Michelle had noticed too.

"Close your eyes, sweetheart."

This time, Rory did what Michelle requested without thinking. Michelle's fingers went straight back to Rory's arm, and Rory began to feel the first sense of nails dragging into her skin. Her eyes opened reflexively. Michelle lifted her chin reprovingly. Rory bit her lip and closed her eyes again. She knew that all she had to do pull away or open her eyes again and that would tell Michelle clearly enough that she wasn't into this.

But she didn't want to. That odd, curious feeling from before suffused her again. Like she didn't need to hold onto her strict control anymore. She didn't have to think about her own sense of self-control when someone was in control for her.

Her eyes remained closed. With the sense of sight removed, all her other senses heightened. She was aware of the steps people took to walk around them in the living room. The tinkling of ice against glass as new drinks were poured. But she was *particularly* aware of the proximity of Michelle to her; the girl's breathing, and—oh god—her touch. Always most important to her awareness were the subtle changes of Michelle's fingers on her. Feathery soft. Sharp. Gentle. Quick. Drawn out.

Rory opened her eyes only a few times, and each of those times met with the same response from Michelle; an abrupt moving away and a sedate reprisal. Rory began to obey Michelle's wishes without question, without feeling an urge to silently dare her.

Michelle's fingers loosened and then let go of Rory wrist. Rory didn't move. The fingers of Michelle's other hand still made a play of the red marks she'd designed up and down the arm. But then fingers were touching the soft flesh of Rory's lips. She gasped, despite herself, a thick intake of breath, shifting the gentle weight of Michelle's fingers against her lips. But she didn't open her eyes.

The reward came a moment later when Michelle's lips replaced her fingers. Rory gave a not subtle moan, abruptly then remembering she was in a room filled with other people. Behind her closed eyes, she winced, and heard Michelle chuckle.

~~*

Back to Coke only, and Rory was chewing a hole in her straw while Michelle had an animated conversation in the kitchen with Katrina and Tobey. She knew she'd be very welcome if she went over there and joined them. But the kitchen was also where the alcohol was. By the same token, she didn't want to seem so needy as to grab Michelle away from a conversation she was enjoying just because she was going nuts on a straw without her.

Maybe it was out of sympathy, or something

else, but Michelle didn't seem to have any more alcohol for the rest of the party either. Had she just had enough earlier in the night and was making sure she was safe to drive, or was it something more?

Thinking about it only drew her around and around in circles, getting no closer to answers.

"It's okay to enjoy it." Brian came over and sat next to her again as if it were the most natural thing in the world. Gemma was reclining on an armchair within hearing distance from them, smiling in the way of so many drunks who had had exactly the right amount of alcohol for the night and were placidly settled in to enjoy the ride.

"That's not—" Rory cut herself off. Brian didn't want to hear about the internal struggle Rory was facing not to get up and add scotch to his Coke. She looked down towards her drink, then back at him as though reconsidering. "It is?"

Brian smiled, and Rory was content with him thinking he'd known what was going on in her mind all along. "She's just giving you space right now. I saw the look in her eyes. She needs to make sure you're okay with it before things go any further, but the middle of a party isn't the time to have that conversation."

"I... know."

Brian looked at her a little bit longer, tipping his head to the side as though he'd realised that he hadn't got it completely right. "You know the whole pleasure and pain thing, yeah? You've come across it before?"

Rory hadn't thought of it in terms of pain, pleasure, or sadomasochism. All she'd thought of was a relief from guilt; an obvious expression of punishment. But Brian's words reframed it, and she found herself nodding. "Yeah. Whips and chains and stuff." She said it with a smile to lighten things. It seemed to have the wrong effect.

"That's not necessarily—" Brian was wide eyed, shaking his head.

"I know." Having put him off balance, Rory felt more at ease. "I've heard of BDSM. There's a club at uni."

"Is there?" Brian's raised eyebrows said he was immediately interested in hearing more about that. "There wasn't when I went." His pout was actually adorable and made him look younger.

Rory decided to help redirect him. "Michelle and I haven't talked about it. This was… a surprise… tonight. Not a bad one!" she was quick to add. *"Just… one we'll need to talk about."*

Brian smirked. "Oh, I'm pretty sure the whole room knew it wasn't a bad one."

"I'm really that transparent?" Rory had been hoping Michelle was overstating it when she told her how responsive Rory could be.

Brian spaced his finger about half an inch away from his thumb. "Just a little bit."

"Humph." But Rory wasn't upset, not really. With the rueful twist still on her lips, she took a moment to survey the room. Another girl had joined the conversation in the kitchen. Gemma hadn't moved. No one showed any signs of congregating closer to her and Brian. Her gaze returned to Brian as she worked up the boldness to ask, "Tell me about it. Your experience?"

"With BDSM?" Brian clarified.

"Yeah."

"What would you like to know about my experience?"

"Well…" Rory realised she wasn't quite sure how to answer that question. "I mean… Are you the dominant, or the submissive?"

Brian's, "Ha!" as she said the word 'dominant' answered that question for her even before he spoke the words, "I'm definitely submissive."

"Okay…" Rory wished desperately for a drink. This would be so much easier—asking personal questions when she hardly even knew Brian—if she had a drink in her hand and her inhibitions somewhere out the window. "Okay, then you can probably answer some stuff that Michelle wouldn't be able to answer."

"Probably," Brian agreed.

Rory nodded. Even so, she still didn't know where to start.

"How about I start?" Brian said, taking sympathy on her. He'd had more than one glass over the night, so at least his inhibitions were at least more compromised than hers.

Rory inclined her head in assent.

"So I came into BDSM at the ripe old age of 25. Gemma and Tobey had been dating for a little while then, but Tobey's definitely not submissive, and Gemma's a switch."

There were two things about that statement that surprised Rory. One, that Brian was now older than 25. But two, "Gemma is dominant? But she seems so… playful."

Again, Rory looked over at the diminutive girl who had danced around the party in the early hours, and was now settled gracelessly in an armchair across from them.

"Appearances can be deceiving." Brian's arch tone said it was not the first time this had been mistaken, and it was something that amused him.

"Go on…" Rory said, giving Gemma another side glance before returning her full attention to Brian.

"I needed a little bit more explaining than you about what BDSM was. What Gemma was into was fine with me, but it never occurred to me that I would enjoy anything like that."

Little did Brian know: it hadn't occurred to Rory that she would enjoy anything like it either! Now that she did, though, it seemed amazing that such a thought had never crossed her mind.

"Anyway, I kept my mind open. Gradually, Gemma and my play in the bedroom advanced and I found…" Brian stopped. He looked at Rory, eyes twinkling in thinly supressed amusement. "Well, we never played in a room full of people, but that might just be a kink that Michelle has that Gemma doesn't."

Rory snorted under her breath. Brian stuck his tongue out, and Rory found a convenient couch cushion to throw at him playfully. This effectively ended their conversation. Rory wasn't quite sure how long they'd been fighting over the couch cushion by the time Michelle walked over. Her stilettos were on her feet again, so she loomed over them. Immediately, Rory ceded the cushion to Brian. She heard, rather than saw, Brian clearing his throat, but Michelle's attention wasn't on him at all.

"Shall we go home?" Michelle asked.

It wasn't really a question. The look in Michelle's eyes said something more than her words. It was the same one she'd worn when they'd been on the couch together. She looked away only briefly to say good night to Brian.

"Have a nice night," he said. It wasn't a subtle suggestion.

Rory corrected the smirk that threatened to twitch on her lips, and the cocky swagger that their conversation prompted. She didn't want to blow this before it had even really begun.

~~*

Unbeknownst to Rory, Michelle had already laid out the same nightie on the bed Rory had worn last time. Rory smiled when she saw it.

Michelle's arms came around her from behind.

"Do you know: I'm captivated by you. The set of your jaw, and cheekbones. They're more obviously pronounced when your eyes are closed. Do you know that?"

Rory shook her head as Michelle turned her around. She felt spellbound by her, rapt.

"They are. Your face is utterly free of its usual animation. Don't get me wrong, I adore how expressive you are."

Michelle kissed her, pulling the other girl towards her to show exactly how this was so. Rory moaned, her back arching towards Michelle. She just wanted to be closer. Michelle ended the kiss before she was ready, but Rory felt patient. She knew already the possibility of reward.

"What did I do to earn your trust so quickly?" Michelle's fingers danced across Rory jawline. This time, there was no need for Rory to keep her eyes closed, to avert them. She had complete view of the naked vulnerability and wonder in Michelle's gaze.

"What did you do?" Rory asked surprised. "You've been kind. Patient. You've accepted my strange behaviour at times without question. You're really good at knowing where my limits are and not pushing past them. Sometimes even without us talking about it. What didn't you do?"

Michelle was happy with this answer; Rory could see that. "I do need to talk to you about some things, though. Are you too tired?" There was a cute little furrow between Michelle's eyebrows that Rory just wanted to kiss away.

"Not even a little bit," Rory answered honestly.

Michelle nodded and, between one moment and the next, her entire expression changed. Cuteness morphed into concern in a way that Rory didn't understand until Michelle next spoke.

"I want to talk about tonight," she said. "I worry that I went too far, too fast—"

To Rory, who'd thought it was just fine at exactly the right pace, she couldn't shake her head fast enough. "Not at all!" If this was taken away, after that one small taste…

But no. Michelle seemed to accept Rory's words at face value. She gave a small, mischievous smile. "Okay. Then we need to have a slightly different talk."

Rory settled down on the edge of the bed, sensing this was not a conversation Michelle wanted to have while they were wrapped around each other. She was right.

"My last relationship ended about a year ago," Michelle said. For the first time since Rory had known her, Michelle was actively avoiding her gaze. "She was my submissive as well as my girlfriend. Towards the end, she said that she didn't want a 'power dynamic', but a 'real relationship', with 'real feelings'. I was shattered. Not the least because that was what I thought I'd been giving her."

"A real relationship with real feelings?" Rory

clarified.

Michelle met Rory's eyes again, and nodded.

Rory swallowed. "Brian and I talked a bit about BDSM tonight," she said, deciding to just come out with it.

"Oh?" Michelle relaxed enough to join Rory on the bed. Their hands found each other, fingers intertwined.

Now it was Rory's turn to feel shy about looking at Michelle as she talked. "There were allusions to your past relationship, but when you were doing that…" Rory drew a finger lightly along Michelle's forearm, and the other girl drew in her breath. It was distracting. Rory found her gaze settling on Michelle's lips, but forced herself to at least finish her sentence. "Well, Brian was surprised that we hadn't talked about this before that."

"Well, alcohol can be liberating that way," Michelle said ruefully.

"Yes it can," Rory said. She pursed her lips. "Is this—BDSM—something you… need, in your relationships?"

Michelle's gaze flashed across to Rory. "I would never force someone into it if they weren't comfortable."

"That's… not what I'm saying." Rory frowned, and struggled to formulate what she was thinking.

"It is something I miss when it's not there," Michelle acknowledged.

Rory could understand that. Definitely. She wet her lips, and noticed the way that drew Michelle's gaze. "It wasn't just the alcohol that made me interested in trying this with you. Would you tell me what it's like? For you? I mean, I know what it means to Brian."

So Michelle did, going into protocol, which was basically giving commands and knowing they would be carried out, light punishments whenever they weren't, mindfulness for both the Dominant and the submissive because it was easy to hurt someone if you were the Dominant, and it was easy to lose yourself and your awareness of your own boundaries if you were the submissive. And Rory began to feel something rising up in her heart, a kind of hope.

They talked until exhaustion could no longer be ignored.

"Come," Michelle said. "There'll be more time to talk tomorrow. Right now, I just want to touch you."

That woke Rory up enough. They went slowly, likely due to Rory's mentioning that this was her first time with a woman. It was different to the way things were in bed with a guy. Pressed against a woman, it was breasts where she had breasts, mounds meeting where she'd only come across flatness before.

There was a moment, after Michelle undressed her, when Rory worried that Michelle would compare Rory's body to her own and find her wanting. But that fear didn't last long. Michelle was skilful with her hands and her lips, and soon Rory wasn't thinking or worrying about anything at all.

Afterwards, Rory lay in Michelle's arms, drawing patterns on skin with her fingertips.

"Does this mean I'm your submissive now?" Rory showed her inexperience in tone as well as words. It may also have been the sleepy tone adding to it. She tried to hide a yawn.

Michelle smirked, then kissed her on the shoulder. "I like the term 'girlfriend'," she said. "But maybe we can look to doing both, if that's something you still want to explore in the morning."

"Maybe we can do both," Rory mumbled in reply.

Chapter Nine

The next morning, Rory woke up before Michelle. She didn't want to wake her but was too restless after everything from the night before to stay in bed. She wandered into the courtyard at the back of the house, her earphones in her ears and a hot cup of instant coffee between her palms, so she didn't hear when Michelle came up behind her.

"How are you doing this morning?" Michelle asked, gently drawing a strand of Rory's wayward blonde hair behind her ear, before coming to sit beside her.

"Good," Rory replied cheerily. But she'd been thinking all morning as well. "I have more questions."

Michelle mockingly gave a groan. "Oh god, what have I done?" she asked woefully, her arms holding onto Rory more tightly.

Rory's reply grin was broad. This was strange, this feeling, so close to the night before when she'd been drinking. And still craving physical contact with the person she'd fallen into bed with the night before. "Your being dominant; doesn't it come out, in little things? Everyday life things. Like taking charge of who pays for our meals?" It had been on her mind, the way that Michelle always stood up from a table first, extended her hand out, compelled Rory to take it.

Michelle looked at Rory for a very long second before replying. "I thought we called that chivalry," she murmured.

"That was before you told me you were a dominant," Rory answered, sassy and unregretful. "Now I'm wondering if there's more to it."

Michelle raised her eyebrows at that, and Rory only narrowly managed to restrain the impulse to poke out her tongue.

"Hmm," was all Michelle said. "I can already see you're going to be trouble."

At that, Rory couldn't help but laugh. It was a sound filled with joy. Rory wanted to take hold of this moment outside between them and keep it with her forever.

Michelle leaned her head against Rory's shoulder. "So what are your questions?"

"Well, like, I'm pretty sure I know the answer to this, but would you always be in charge if we did this? Or would I get to have my say? Like, in front of friends and stuff. I don't necessarily want everyone to know… Not that I'd be ashamed…!" Rory's words stumbled to a stop and she realised she hadn't thought through the question well enough.

"Because it's not necessarily anyone's business," Michelle said, nodding against Rory's shoulder. "Like sex. You wouldn't necessarily do that in front of friends either. I'm sorry," she added then.

"What?"

"For last night. I shouldn't have done that. If I'd been sober, I wouldn't have, not without talking about it with you first. Not that that's an excuse." Michelle lifted her head from Rory's shoulder and looked at her directly. Her glasses were slightly skewed from being pressed against Rory's shoulder. "Do you think you can forgive me for that?"

"Oh, sweetheart..." It warmed Rory that Michelle felt the need to apologise for the night before, for anything taken without permission, and her forgiveness was given immediately because of it. "Of course. Thank you." She lifted her arm and Michelle curled in close to her again.

~~*

It was Monday before Rory returned back to her own place, still wearing the same clothes she'd left with on Friday.

"Oh, you're back." Helena's eyebrows rose towards her hairline even as, a moment later, she turned back to her laptop in an attempt not to make a big deal of it.

Rory didn't say anything, just grabbed new clothing and went to the shower.

When she came back, Helena hadn't moved.

Rory wondered whether she'd been sitting there like that all weekend, and suddenly realised she didn't know very much about what Helena did in her personal life lately.

"What did you get up to this weekend?" Rory asked, throwing a towel over her shoulder and starting the process of drying her hair.

"Nothing all that interesting," Helena said.

Rory didn't really know how to answer that closed statement, so she just nodded. A moment later, she got up again to pull out her laptop and make an update on Facebook.

"It's just, I'm not your mum to ask you where you're going or wonder where you've been," Helena said out of nowhere.

Rory pushed her laptop lid down to halfway so she could see Helena over it. "I know that," she said slowly.

"It's just," Helena said again, "if I had been you, I would have wanted new clean clothes before now."

"I borrowed Michelle's clothes in between," Rory murmured.

"Oh."

It was awkward. It was awkward, and Rory didn't know why. Surely her dating another girl wasn't enough to cause this much reaction from her housemate. She'd known Helena wasn't completely comfortable about it the last time they talked, but this was something else. She tried again to go back to her laptop when Helena didn't say anything else immediately after but, again, the girl started speaking as soon as she lost Rory attention.

"I just don't understand it."

Rory sighed. "Understand *what*?" she asked.

"Understand how you can just... meet someone. And be so happy. You make it look so easy."

Rory thought over the weekend. Having Michelle in her life was the easiest thing there was. "Why shouldn't it be easy?" she asked Helena.

"Because!" But even Helena seemed to know that was no kind of answer. "Because what about when it all goes wrong? What about when the person you love doesn't go to your uni anymore, and you don't seem to have anything in common anymore, even though he promised that wasn't going to happen, and you spend all Saturday night waiting by the phone because even one text message will vindicate the decision not to go out—"

"Okay, stop." Rory put aside her laptop and ended Helena's rambling outburst by giving Helena her full attention.

Helena's eyes were glistening with unshed tears. "How is worth it when you don't know that you won't just be strangers sharing a common past in another month's time?" she demanded softly.

None of this was anything to do with Rory new relationship with Michelle, Rory realised. She should have known that, should have been able to give Helena the benefit of the doubt. The whole world didn't revolve around who Rory was dating.

"I'm just. So. Lonely," Helena whispered. "And, with you never here anymore, I feel like I'm the one that something's wrong with, the one nobody wants to be around."

"Helena…" Rory didn't know what to say to that. She was so used to feeling that herself. Realising her housemate felt the same way, even without a drinking problem, froze the words in Rory's mouth.

Helena gave up on the battle against tears when she wiped her sleeve across the face her feelings were written on. "I'm sorry. This isn't your problem. I'm sorry."

"Don't be sorry," Rory said. "I'm sorry," she said, able to find words again in the face of her housemate's tears. "I've felt that way too. Really recently."

"You have?" There was something like hope in Helena's expression, which made Rory feel even sadder.

"I have," she confirmed. "I know what it feels like. And I'm sorry you feel that way. I'm sorry I've been out so often. Look, it's the end of semester soon. Michelle's putting together a little dinner to celebrate it. Just her and me and a few people she's introduced me to. Would you like to come?" It wouldn't have occurred to Rory to have

Helena there before now, but the more she thought about it—especially in the light of finding out Helena wasn't actually weirded out that Rory had a girlfriend—the more she warmed to the idea.

A watery smile gazed up at her from the couch. "Are you sure that would be all right?" Helena asked.

"It's my party. I'm pretty sure I can invite whomever I want. I'd like you there."

The hope and hint of happiness that shone behind the tears in Helena's eyes were proof enough that it was the right thing.

~~*

Rory texted Michelle on the way to AA that night to as if she could add another person when she made the reservation.

She still felt strongly about her continued routine of going to group. She didn't really understand what had happened over the weekend, and she really didn't want to relapse just because she got cocky and thought she was on top of it when she wasn't actually. Yes, she had had one drink and then stopped there. But Michelle had been instrumental in her stopping at that point, not Rory herself.

As usual, there was the period of time after the facilitator stopped talking when the room subsided into silence and nobody looked at each other. This time, Rory was the first one to speak.

"I drank on the weekend. But then… something happened. Something that made me stop. Drinking, I mean. Before I went too far. Have any of you ever successfully found something that distracts you from unhelpful behaviour at parties before it all starts going really wrong?"

Rory looked around the room. There wasn't a big group there tonight. Some of the regulars, one or two new people. From them, there were mostly non-committal murmurs and shrugs. One of the men spoke about his wife's strength in supporting him whenever things got that hard. Rory waited patiently as he offered his story. But she knew it was nothing like what she'd experienced with Michelle on the weekend well before he finished. How could it be? What he was describing was a normal marital interaction.

Apart from the people at Gemma's party, and the club at uni, she'd hardly even heard of people who talked about BDSM, let alone BDSM curing alcoholism.

At least for a little while. Long enough that she might feel able to breathe again.

Rory supposed she hadn't really been expecting any of the people at group to open up about BDSM and its practical applications towards helping people not to drink; that was far too specific. But even if she hadn't been expecting it, that hadn't stopped her from kind of hoping to find someone here to talk it over with.

When everyone else stopped talking, Rory bowed her head and tried to explain it for herself. "I was at a party at the weekend. I know, it was stupid to tempt myself, but there I was, offered a drink, which I accepted like an idiot." She paused here, aware that she was using humour as a way of dampening the sickened emotions she felt at her own behaviour; aware that it wasn't working and the tears were welling up despite herself.

This was important to do, she reminded herself. It wasn't healthy for her to go on feeling she'd been fine. This was the truth as well. She'd accepted a drink before Michelle had come over. Rory gave herself a moment, and blinked them back, before continuing.

"The usual pattern should have started up after that. One drink leading to another, to another, and another. But it didn't. The girl I've been… seeing managed to turn it around…" She'd hesitated there, because she was sure that someone would speak out, would point out that she wasn't supposed to be starting any new relationships right now.

But no one did.

The man who'd shared the story about his wife's strength started nodding in understanding. Rory felt like she was telling it wrong.

"I…"

Close your eyes, sweetheart.

The words were there, available for her to use, but she didn't feel comfortable in sharing something so personal. She wasn't sure yet what it all meant between her and Michelle. One conversation and a weekend wasn't enough to sort through all those questions. She didn't feel ready to share it with everyone else until she knew what it meant herself.

Hmm. I can already see you're going to be trouble.

Rory cleared her throat, changing the direction of her sharing at the last minute. "I guess that was… quite a relief for me," she said, ducking her head into her hand. She saw a room full of supportive faces before she ducked her head. For the first time, she didn't feel like she was getting anything out of any of it.

At the mid-time break, Rory was the first person to leave the room for the kitchen, running a hand through her hair and not caring how that dishevelled it. She didn't turn around to face the rest of the people who were coming out for the free tea and coffee; didn't have any kind of façade back in place. The dark reflection of herself in the window seemed wan and sad.

"How have you been going?"

For a moment, Rory tried to believe the man behind her wasn't speaking to her. One breath, then two, and she turned around with a fragile smile pasted to her face. It was the man who was not too much older than her, the one who had only spoken up on her first night here.

"Sounds like you had a pretty good week, all things considered," he continued. "Jason," he said, pointing his fingers to his chest to remind her of a name she had surely only heard once if at all.

"Right." Rory nodded jerkily. She just didn't have it in her to pretend, all over again, that the conversation in there had gone exactly the way she wanted it to.

"So, things are getting better? Slowly?" Jason tipped his head to the side, brown eyes looking at her with some compassion as his smile slipped down a couple of notches.

Rory gazed away from him, fixing on a corner in the room and slowly shaking her head. It was the closest she could come to admission, and even that brought tears dangerously close to her eyes.

Jason frowned, but he didn't reach out to touch her. There were rules about personal boundaries that people were good about keeping aware of. "Did… did you want to step outside?"

Still not looking at him, Rory nodded.

Stepping outside, Rory fixed her eyes to the concrete beneath her feet, noting the sound of the click of the door closing—not locking—behind Jason. There was a small circle of light around them on the patio. People inside wouldn't be unaware that they'd gone, or where.

"Sorry," she murmured, speaking to the concrete, and to Jason.

"Jesus, you're apologising to me. You don't need to apologise to me. I'm sorry for whatever I said."

Rory shrugged, disheartened.

The two of them stood in silence for a long while. Rory saw the way Jason's feet shuffled in front of her, like he was uncertain how to approach her now that they were here.

"You can go inside if you want," she mumbled.

One of Jason's feet took half a step back. "I can get a facilitator for you. If that would be better?"

Rory didn't want a facilitator. Not after the way the discussion had just gone. "Please, no…"

Another foot shuffle. Then, "Was it something in there that set you off?" Jason asked quietly.

Rory sniffed. Then realised she had to answer. It was outright rude to make him feel like he couldn't leave and then not say anything when he tried to help. "I feel like nobody understands."

Jason was quiet for a while, possibly considering how he wanted to reply, then, "This group is an older demographic than some. You have the occasional kid who comes in, and some people around our age. I find it… helpful, looking at older people who have gone through this and trying to learn from them. But I understand how it could be isolating."

To hear someone articulating a reason—any reason—behind what she was feeling was so liberating she almost smiled. Almost.

"Helpful, you say?" Rory asked, taking a breath and looking up at him.

"Well, yeah." A small dimple showed up in Jason's left cheek. "Keeps it in perspective why I'm choosing not to drink."

Chapter Ten

"I've been going to meetings."

They were in his place, somewhere he shared off campus with two other guys. Thankfully, neither of them were home in the middle of the weekday afternoon. Smithy had ushered her away and Rory—feeling too drained to fight anymore—let him take her.

"I've known there's a problem for a while now," she murmured, staring at her hands, at the cup of tea she held between them.

Smithy held one too. "It's soothing," he'd said when he suggested he pour one for each of them.

Since Rory wasn't screaming or crying at him anymore, she supposed that was an improvement. Smithy's lips were pursed in what she supposed was sympathy, or the effort to keep from speaking over her.

"I suppose you can't argue that there's not a problem when, every time you go to a meeting, you have to admit that you've had a drink in between times." Looking into the tea as though it had some answers for her problem, Rory shook her head. She felt too ashamed to look up at him. At yet, there was a precious pleasure in the pain of admitting these things out loud. "You were totally right when you thought something was up. When we had dinner. But it isn't something you need to feel bad about." If she was going to go through the pain of doing this, she needed to get it all out. "It would have been the same regardless of if you were there or not."

It was hard to say. It didn't change anything and it didn't make her feel better like she'd hoped it might. Finally, she dared a look up at Smithy to see what he thought of her.

The frown that had travelled low on his brows had smoothed. He looked… lighter. As he caught her looking at him, he even gave her a small, reassuring smile. And Rory suddenly felt… better. Like she'd hoped.

She heaved a long sigh, and smiled back to him. "Wow, this honesty thing is hard." Her voice shook and she tried to make it sound like it was due to a self-deprecating laugh.

"Well, if it helps, I think you're doing really well."

"Oh. Good." Rory ducked her head, unable to keep meeting his frank gaze. Her throat felt raw from crying, and she told herself she deserved it. It was just another punishment. "Especially since you're the one I just yelled at."

"It is good, actually." Smithy let her keep her gaze on her tea while he spoke to her. "I've been making myself sick about how I handled that night we went out to dinner. I can't count the number of fights me and Tally have had. I didn't say anything!" he said quickly when Rory gaze flashed back up to him, "About you. About what I thought you were dealing with."

"Thanks," Rory said quietly, returning her gaze to her hands. If it was bad having Smithy know about her, the idea of Tally knowing was even worse.

"Well, yeah, because I wasn't sure it really was what you were dealing with."

"Yeah."

"Yeah."

"Will it be bad for you now?" she dared to ask him. "You know… what I am for real now. Will it be bad keeping that from Tally? I don't… I don't want her to know." Her whole body shied away from the idea of her knowing, pressing itself back further into her chair.

"It's not my story to tell," Smithy told her simply.

She nodded her head a couple of times. A part of her wished he hadn't pushed her in her confession. There were still remains of the part of her who wanted to hide this knowledge from everyone else.

"I've been spending all this time trying to hide it. From everyone. I feel like, if I spent that time fighting the problem instead, I'd be doing a better job." She gave another sigh, as though muscling herself up for more honesty. "I'm an idiot. Such an idiot." She lifted her gaze, hoping that there would still be the understanding there he'd shown before she was ready to hear it.

"The hardest thing is accepting it," Smithy said. His voice was low pitched and gentle, eyes kind. "That's what my cousin said anyway."

Rory felt a flooding of relief. There was nothing judgemental about his tone or body language, and Rory appreciated so much that she could relax here and talk with him about this. She almost started crying again.

Thankfully, Smithy didn't seem to get scared in the face of a crying girl. It was for herself, then, rather than him, that she tried to keep her eyes clear and any tears left from earlier unshed.

When she was sure she could go on, she said, "I don't suppose your cousin had any tips for how to go from there?"

"He did, actually," Smithy said. "Take each day one at a time. It's like eating the elephant."

A laugh choked out of Rory at the absurdity of that. When Smithy didn't laugh with her, she coughed, then asked, "Eating the what?"

"The elephant," Smith answered, as though it wasn't ridiculous. "It's too big to think of eating the whole elephant at once. So you take it one bite at a time. Turn it into small, manageable pieces."

Rory had to admit, when he put it like that, it didn't sound so crazy.

Thinking about days in terms of weeks or months would likewise get overwhelming. How much easier was it for Rory to think of not having a drink for the rest of the day, rather than the rest of the week, or month?

"You don't have to battle this alone, you know," Smithy told her. "You do know that, right?"

Rory considered it. "I didn't," she said slowly, "but I think I'm starting to now. Thank you," Rory said. "I mean, thanks. I mean, again."

"It's the least I can do." Now it was Smithy who sounded self-deprecating. "I mean, I did push you into talking about this before you were ready."

"I was going to point that out," Rory said, pointing to him. "You owe me now."

Smithy's eyebrows raised, and another smile crossed his lips. "Is that so?"

Rory shrugged. "Well, maybe this conversation will even the score."

"And we're keeping score now!"

The words could have sounded affronted, but it was impossible to take it that way when Smithy's face rested in such a ludicrous expression.

Rory only just stopped herself from saying 'thank you' again, and settled instead for a small, under-the-breath chuckle.

"Smithy…" She turned hesitant as she wondered: had she maybe accidentally found the person with whom she could talk about the things she hadn't been able to bring up in her last support group.

"Mmm?"

"Can I… ask something? Something that might sound potentially crazy?"

Smithy gave her a look. He glanced around the room and the space between them pointedly. "I don't know if you're in the same conversation I'm in, but this is pretty crazy."

"Point," Rory acceded. She took a deep breath, then let it out again. "Okay. Have you heard of BDSM?"

In for a penny, in for a pound. She didn't see a point in drawing it out now that he'd given her permission to ask.

"Yes?" Whatever he'd been expecting, it clearly hadn't been this. "Why?"

"Well…" So much for in for a pound; Rory suddenly felt nervous again about bringing up this whole conversation with him. "Okay, so it's like this: I was at a party last weekend. A party where there were people drinking. And, like I said, the result should have been the same regardless of if who was there, and what was happening."

Smithy was nodding along. It appeared he'd gone back to silence in favour of letting her speak.

"Okay. So it should have been that way. Except, it wasn't."

Smithy narrowed his eyes. Rory could see the way he tried to connect the story she was telling with the BDSM she had asked about earlier. She tried to get into telling that from a different direction.

"I've been seeing this girl for a while." Rory expected something from Smithy, but his facial expression didn't change. "Dating her, actually," she added, in case he didn't understand.

"Okay," Smithy said when it became clear that she expected some response.

Rory looked at him for a long time but when he became obvious that he had nothing more to say, Rory wondered if she'd been the strange one for expecting more of a reaction from him.

"Okay," she repeated. Her mind veered away from the word 'alcoholic' even as she thought it. Words poured out of her, trying to cover that awful one. "So, I was standing in the kitchen. I'd just been poured a second drink. And Michelle came up…"

Rory's words drifted off as her mind brought that moment back, thought of the words Michelle had said, how she'd said them so matter of fact.

I don't think that's a good idea.

It hadn't just been the words. It had been the way she'd said them. The look in Michelle's eyes. She hadn't taken the drink away from her; hadn't needed to.

Smithy's eyebrows drew low to the bridge of his nose as Rory explained this to him. He kept his gaze concentrated on her as he sought to understand the situation she was describing.

"Even before I knew what it meant, I responded to something in Michelle's posture, like she would be… Disappointed isn't the right word." Rory frowned as she struggled to find the right word.

"Disapproving?" Smithy asked.

"No. I mean, maybe." Rory's lips twisted. "I didn't understand it myself until later on in the night. She kept me distracted. Made sure my whole attention was on her. It was like, when I gave up my drink because she'd suggested it, I handed over control. She was in control. And I didn't drink again that night."

Rory gaze beseeched Smithy to understand; to understand it all, if possible, but especially that last part.

Smithy took a couple of moments, breaking eye contact and nodding as he sorted through what she'd told him.

"That sounds… I mean, good comes to mind. You didn't drink again. But." Smithy frowned.

Then Rory frowned. This wasn't what she'd been expecting. She'd opened this up expecting a debrief and a celebration that she'd found something that worked. Smithy was acting like she'd told him something bad.

"Having someone else in control doesn't help you with your problem," Smithy said heavily. "It just puts dealing with it off. What happens if you stop dating Michelle?"

Rory hadn't thought of that. She was struck dumb for several moments.

"I'm sorry."

Devastation must have shown on her face. For

the first time, Smithy reached out to touch her. Rory reminded herself to breathe normally, trying to swallow past a throat that suddenly seemed choked up. Her fingers felt like they had pins and needles, and she hardly felt it when Smithy's larger hand enveloped hers.

"I didn't mean to..." Smithy wiped his free hand across his mouth and looked away as though looking at her was too awful. "I just didn't want you to go from not coping at all to finding a coping mechanism that was equally unsustainable," he told the wall.

If she'd been herself, she might have mocked him for using such a large word. But Rory felt like she was separate from herself, floating above them both and watching dispassionately as this addiction happened to someone else.

"Rory? Rory..." Smithy was shaking her hand with his, and Rory realised abruptly that she'd started to cry again. It didn't feel like anything, this crying. Wasn't like before where she'd been screaming and wailing. She felt numb.

But she knew she still had to respond to him. "I'm here," she said, blinking several times before focusing on him. "I'm okay."

It was a lie and they both knew it, but Smithy removed his hand and sat back on the couch across from her. Again, he wiped his hand over his mouth. Rory wondered distantly if that was a usual nervous tick for him, or if it was something that had been created because of her.

She didn't know how to continue from here. Gazing back into her mug, she realised that at some point she'd finished the tea. "I should go," she said, standing.

Smithy stood too. His arms seemed gangly at his sides; clearly he had no idea what to do with them. "You don't need to…" he started.

"I should." She put the cup that had been clenched between her hands down on the table deliberately and turned to go.

"Rory." Out of some passive sense of politeness, she turned back towards his call. "I understand if you don't want to speak to me anymore. And I'll do my best to keep Tally off your back. No promises there. But… well…" He took a scrap of paper out of his back pocket, fumbled around until he found a pen, and wrote something on it. "I'm here for you, all right? I may not always say the right thing, but I'm here. Not just at parties, but really in real life. Here."

He handed her the piece of paper, and Rory took it in numb fingers.

"You've got my number now," he said, making sure to tilt his head so that he could meet her eyes. "We can catch up whenever."

"Thanks," Rory said one last time around the thickness in her throat.

Chapter Eleven

Rory sat at her desk in her room and stared at the computer screen. She'd been sitting this way for three quarters of an hour. The cursor of the word document blinked before a blank document. Rory didn't have the impetus to argue or write for any of her assignments. But she couldn't quite bring herself to turn off the computer and walk away. Walking away would mean failing, and she just didn't think she could deal with failing in another area right now.

Instead of writing her essay, Rory thought about that exchange of control, and what it had meant to her. Clearly, Michelle taking control over the situation, at its base, had meant that Rory had no need to decide whether or not she would drink. It had been difficult, but under Michelle's touch, there had never been a genuine threat that she would choose to drink over her interactions with her girlfriend.

Had there?

No. But how much had that to do with the BDSM element of exchange of control, and how much to do with not wanting to disappoint another person. She was already so disappointed in herself; she knew how that felt. She knew she didn't want to feel that from another person. Wasn't that the reason she'd avoided her mum's phone calls until Daphne had simply stopped ringing?

Rory turned off her computer screen and swivelled away from it on her desk chair, no longer even pretending that she was getting done any university homework.

But just because Michelle was another person she didn't want to disappoint didn't mean that her girlfriend was a person who could fix her problems for her. Rory would be doing them both a disservice if she ever viewed her that way. The only one who could fix her problems was Rory.

She didn't deserve punishment, whether that came in the form of BDSM, of a sore throat that was raw from crying. She deserved to get better.

Her phone rang, and the display read 'Michelle'. Rory watched the phone without answering until the display read '1 Missed Call' and Michelle left a voicemail.

"Hi sweetie, just calling in to check on how you've been doing since the weekend. Give me a call when you get this."

Rory put the phone back on her desk. She didn't call Michelle back immediately. Instead, she looked back to blank computer screen and thought what she, Rory, was going to do about her situation next.

Her phone rang again. Rory blinked, surprised to find another half hour had gone by. This time, it was her mum. Apparently, she hadn't completely stopped ringing after all.

Rory stared at the phone display, reminding herself to breathe. She let it ring several times before reaching out with a sharp movement. She wasn't sure whether she was going to pick it up or disconnect the call until she answered it.

"Rory? Oh, it's good to get hold of you. I thought I was going to be leaving another voicemail."

"No, you caught me." Rory lifted the corners of her lips in a smile she didn't feel. She'd heard somewhere that, if a person smiled while they were speaking, a person would be able to hear the smile in the voice.

That didn't work in this case. "Rory? What's wrong, love?"

Rory's breath hitched. "What do you mean, 'what's wrong'?"

"You sound... I don't know. Have you got a cold?"

Rory rasped out a laugh with the same sincerity as her prior smile. "No. I don't have a cold. I have a—" A problem, Rory had been going to say, but her throat closed again before she could get it out. Her mouth moved, trying to form the word without the sound.

"Sweetheart?" Daphne sounded more concerned now.

"I do have something to tell you," Rory said hurriedly, trying to get around the subject a different way. She'd read the twelve steps to recovery. The first step was admitting that she had a problem, that she was powerless when it came to alcohol. If she couldn't tell her mum, how was she ever going to tell the truth to Michelle? "Do you mind if I tell you in person?"

"Rory, is this something I need to worry about?" Daphne asked her slowly.

"No," Rory lied. "I'm fine. I just need to tell you something. Just, not over the phone."

"All right." There was still a note in Daphne's voice that told her she was free to change her mind if she wanted to, but she didn't push. "You tell me when you're ready. I'll be here for you. You know that."

"I know that." Rory cut herself off before tears thickened her throat. She cleared it, then said, "I have an assignment I need to get finished. Could we catch up… one night next week?"

~~*

It was the end of the last day of semester. Winter had well and truly settled into Melbourne, with leaves having fallen off most of the trees and only the occasional day of sun. Rory and Helena were ready for the celebration Michelle had planned. She'd insisted on picking the girls up at the door even though Helena was coming with them, and it wasn't technically a date.

Michelle arrived on time, and Helena was the

one nearest to the door when she knocked.

"I'm Michelle. You must be Helena," she greeted warmly.

"Nice to meet you," Helena said, opening the door wider and stepping back so that Michelle could come into their little home.

"I've heard so much about you."

"Good things, I hope," Michelle answered, winking at Rory with the complete lack of worry of someone who felt secure in her relationship.

Rory watched as Michelle walked into her space. She was standing right next to the couch, a small curve to her lips.

"What's that smirk for?" Michelle asked. Her hips sashayed as she crossed the room, touching her lightly at the waist before their lips touched.

"This is the first time you've been in my living room," Rory said. She liked the way that Michelle filled out the space. Liked the way that there were no signs of the weirdness from Helena. Liked how comfortable it all felt.

Helena snuck off into the bathroom before they left, and Michelle snuck another none-too-subtle kiss from Rory. "We'll have to make a habit of it," she said. Her voice was sultry and low, which had the added side effect of masking what they were saying from Helena while she was in the bathroom.

The toilet flushed and Rory felt a little bit of self-consciousness. Even if Helena hadn't been actively weird since Michelle walked in, she didn't want to sit virtually on top of Michelle when she walked out of the bathroom.

Michelle seemed to catch onto the train of thought, and so the two of them had shoes on and were ready to leave by the time the bathroom door opened and Helena stepped out.

The conversation on the way to the restaurant was largely carried by Michelle and Helena. Michelle was inclusive and friendly. Rory stayed quiet, not wanting to do or say anything that would ruin the easy camaraderie between the two women. It was a short drive. When they arrived, they were the first people escorted to the table Michelle had reserved.

"First round of drinks," Michelle said, as she lifted her hand to wave a waiter over. "My shout. What would you like?"

"Are you sure you don't mind?" Helena asked.

"Ask Rory if I mind," Michelle said.

Rory snorted, remembering the conversations they'd had about Michelle paying for food and drinks whenever they went out. "She doesn't mind," Rory told Helena, even while her eyes stayed on Michelle.

"Well, if you really don't mind, I'll grab a cider," Helena said, still sounding uncertain.

"A cider for this lady, please," said Michelle, "and for Rory…?"

"Just a lemonade for me," she said, gazing up towards the waiter.

"A lemonade, and a glass of red wine for me,"

Michelle told the waiter.

Brian walked in not too long afterwards, followed by Gemma and Tobey. Over the next moments, Rory and Michelle greeted her friends with excitement, introducing them to Helena as they sat across from her.

"Good to see you again," Brian said, giving Rory a hug from behind her seat taking the last free chair across from her.

"I guess congratulations for end of semester are due to you as well, Helena," Gemma said, raising a glass in salute.

Michelle moved her hand from Rory leg to reach for her hand. Under the table, their hands dangled. Rory managed to smile comfortably and order another lemon squash when the waiter came around to get a second round of drink orders and the meals.

"Aurora?"

Rory pulled her hand away from Michelle's reflexively. Only one person called her that, despite Rory's repeated attempts to get her to stop. Michelle looked at her curiously, before turning her head in the direction of the call. Rory desperately wanted to grab Michelle so that her girlfriend couldn't look anywhere that wasn't her.

"Aurora! It is you!"

There was no way around this.

It seemed like it was in slow motion that Rory turned around to face Tally.

"Hey, how're you going?" she asked weakly.

"Good, good." Tally was smiling but Smithy was behind her. The expression on his face was grim. When Rory met his eyes, he shook his head slightly, and Rory felt like she needed to bolt. But then she wouldn't be here to curb whatever Tally was about to say. She watched as Tally nodded to her housemate. "Oh hey, I know you. Helena, isn't it?"

Helena nodded her head dumbly, not seeming sure what to make of the friendly words couched in such a bitter tone.

"So, this is an end of semester party?" she asked.

"It is," said Helena. She looked at Rory, then Michelle, as if in question. Rory could almost see the question: *Wait, aren't you guys friends?* written across her housemate's features.

The smile on Michelle's painted lips was guarded. She didn't have all the answers Rory had, but she looked again to Rory before crinkling the corners of her eyes at Tally. She clearly knew something was up, just not what.

"Well that's fantastic." Tally reached behind her to hit Smithy lightly on the stomach. "Isn't that great, Smithy?"

"Yeah," Smithy said. "You know, we should probably go. If we want to get served—"

"What *I* want to know is that, if *our Aurora* was having a party, why didn't we get invited?"

Rory flinched every time Tally used that name, but she wouldn't say anything—couldn't say anything—without causing a scene.

Tally tapped her lips with one finger. The nail was bit almost to the quick, and wasn't painted. Here it came, Rory knew; another guilt trip about how she'd been avoiding Tally. "I mean, we're your friends, aren't we? I mean, your number is in Smithy's phone. Did you know that. Oh! Of course you knew that. You guys have been texting each other."

They had been. Rory gaze flashed to Smithy's as she realised the kind of content that Tally would have read if she'd gone through their recent phone text messages.

"No…" She breathed the word. The ambient noise of the restaurant almost drowned out her voice, but she could see Michelle heard it.

"Okay." Michelle straightened in her seat protectively so that, even though Tally was standing taller than her, Michelle possessed the more commanding stature. "I think your friend there's right. You should probably go." There was still a pleasant smile on her lips, but her eyes were cold now, intent.

Rory held out the hope that whatever she felt when Michelle took on that stature would affect Tally.

No such luck. Tally's lips twisted in a parody of a smile as she finally looked at Michelle. "You think you're so important. Did she tell you that you were special? That you were the first girl she ever had feelings for?" There was a sneer in her voice, but that wasn't what made Rory wilt.

She had said that. She'd said exactly those words. Michelle gave another quick side glance her way, and Rory shrank into herself just a little bit more. But surely Michelle wouldn't think… wouldn't think…

Tally's lips stretched with grim pleasure at the sideways look between them. "Wait till Rory finds the next girl she's interested in and chooses to forget about you," she crooned.

"You know what?" Gemma said suddenly. "Love isn't something you have to give to one person. Sometimes people forget other people because they're just unpleasant." She crossed her arms over her chest, looking annoyed at Tally, but pleased with herself.

"So we're not even friends anymore. Is that how it is?" Tally glared daggers at Rory. "You're still friends with *my boyfriend*, but not with me."

"Tally…" Rory started.

"No, you're right," Tally said. "I'm sure this is all incredibly awkward for you and your new friends."

Rory noticed how Tally deliberately didn't look at Gemma anymore when she spoke.

"Well, you know what? Now that we're not playing friends anymore, I just want you to know that I see right through you." She bared her teeth at Rory. Rory tried not to recoil. "I've walked with you through your best dreams and seen what's in them. I know how scared you are of drinking again, of turning into an alcoholic."

Rory heart stopped at the word spoken out loud. She felt sick, but Tally wasn't done.

"You think it's bad now. But you'll drink again."

"That's enough," Michelle said suddenly, and sharply. She pushed her chair back violently enough that it almost toppled over, and she actually towered over Tally. "Go home," she told Tally. Her gaze lifted to Smithy. Her voice brooked no argument. "Take her home. Now."

"Come on, Tally," Smithy said in a smaller voice. He looked pale too, Rory noticed, but she didn't know what to do with that knowledge.

Tally might have argued, might have said that they hadn't got the food they'd come here for. But she'd done the damage already. She'd said what she'd come here to say, neatly sweeping in and taking care of it before Rory had a chance to.

Rory found she was shaking. Tally was escorted away. Even in the other girl's absence, Rory didn't dare look up at anyone else at the rest of the table.

Their meals arrived, but Rory wasn't hungry.

Chapter Twelve

"I'm… just gonna give you guys some space," Helena said. She'd driven back from the restaurant with them, in the backseat of Michelle's car. She hadn't said a word until now. Then, in an even smaller voice, she added, "I'll be… out."

Michelle and Rory were silent for several minutes after Helena closed the door softly behind her.

Rory didn't know how to begin. She was scared that, if one of them didn't say something soon, both of them would be stuck in this silence until Helena came back.

"Okay," Michelle said finally, and Rory felt giddy with relief. At least until her next words. "I don't want to hear it from a disgruntled ex… or…" Michelle shook her head and met gazes with Rory, "whatever Tally is. I want to hear things in your words."

Having said her piece, she sat down on Rory computer chair with the air of someone who was done with speaking, at least until her request was met.

Rory took a couple of backward steps until her legs hit the side of the bed. She collapsed onto the mattress weakly. "Okay." There were two things that Michelle had asked her, and Rory wanted to address them both. "Tally's not my ex. She's not *my* anything."

Rory's hands were shaking. She pressed them against the mattress beside her thighs and pretended not to notice them; was keenly aware that Michelle's sharp eyes missed so very little.

"She's right, though." And here Rory faltered. She hadn't been ready to tell Michelle yet, but the situation had forced her into it. She had no choice but to respond to Tally's accusations now. So she forced herself not to shy away from it. "I'm afraid to drink."

Rory closed her eyes and opened them again before the fear and angst of what she was saying overwhelmed her and sealed her lips.

"So that's the big secret I've been keeping from everyone. In between uni and seeing you, I've been going to meetings. I've been telling total strangers my fears in the hope that they'll be able to fix me." Once she started, she continued almost by rote, saying the same words that she'd said to Smithy over a week before. She found that it was harder to meet Michelle's eyes. It wasn't easier having already had this conversation with Smithy. She had so much more to lose with Michelle.

She dared a glance at her girlfriend. Her face was impassive. Rory didn't know how to read it without her fears intruding.

Michelle waited patiently.

"I was ashamed. That's why I didn't tell you. And being with you has been so much fun! I didn't want to do or say anything that might make that end. I may have kissed Tally when we were both drunk, but I—"

Rory cut herself off, reframed what she'd been about to say, and tried again.

"It is different with you. And new for me. I've never had anything like this. That's why I told you that you were the first woman I kissed. You *were* the first woman I kissed when I was fully aware of making that decision." A pleading note had entered Rory's voice. She didn't like it, but she so desperately wanted Michelle to understand; was so desperately worried that she wouldn't. "I hardly remember anything that happened with Tally, I was so drunk. And I'm ashamed of that. So I kept things from you. And that was stupid."

"It was."

Like Smithy, Michelle didn't merely mouth whatever she thought Rory wanted to hear. Rory tried to take hope in that; like they were still able to talk honestly to each other and it was still worth it to try.

"Because you kept this from me, I took you to a party where there was alcohol," Michelle continued, from between thin lips. Her voice was cool, disappointed. "Where you drank alcohol."

"And then you stopped me from drinking more," Rory reminded her, before adding in a mumble, "I thought you knew about it then."

Michelle shook her head with a foul bark of laughter; possibly the most indelicate sound Rory had ever heard from her. "I had been drinking, and I was stupid enough to forget myself and engage in a power play even though I hadn't talked it over with you first."

"We talked about that."

"Oh, I know. Thank god you didn't mind. But this..." Michelle shook her head. "I thought you trusted me."

"I do," Rory said. Then again with more feeling, "I *do* trust you."

Michelle looked at Rory silently. The words were in the air between them. *If you trusted me, why didn't you tell me this?*

Thank god, she didn't actually say them out loud.

"I need to think about what you keeping this quiet means to me. I don't want to abandon you. But I need some... time," Michelle said with finality.

"Time," Rory echoed numbly.

Michelle nodded, as though hearing Rory say it strengthened her resolve. But when she looked at Rory, and really saw her again, her face did soften.

"You're dealing with a very difficult thing, and I trust that you've been battling with it the best way you know how. This isn't goodbye," Michelle told Rory forcefully, putting her hand against Rory's cheek and making sure she didn't shy away as she so desperately wanted to. "You've had longer to think about this than I have. I'm just asking for a day or two to process."

Rory just nodded her head, not trusting herself to speak yet.

Michelle's dark lashes lowered over her eyes for a moment then in one, two, three strides, Michelle held Rory in her arms, and was lifting her chin to find and kiss her lips.

Rory grasped to Michelle as though she was in very real danger of sinking, but Michelle only allowed them that small goodbye kiss before she pulled away and strode to the door, opening and then shutting it quietly behind her.

In her absence, Rory felt all the air deflate from her. This wasn't how the night was supposed to have gone. This wasn't how any of it was supposed to have gone.

~~*

Helena knocked so lightly on Rory's door when she came back that Rory almost didn't hear. She looked up when Helena pushed open the door ever so slightly.

"Is it safe to come in?" she asked quietly.

Rory remained curled up on her bed, not looking at anything.

"She's not here," she told Helena dully.

Helena came into the room and closed the door behind her just as gently as Michelle had.

Rory had no idea how much time had lapsed since Michelle left. She didn't move as the end of the bed dipped, and Helena sat there. She didn't have the heart to have the same conversation with her housemate that she'd had with Michelle, even though both girls had heard what Tally had had to say that night.

Rory would have killed to have a drink right then. Several drinks. A whole bottle of scotch didn't even seem outlandish. If Smithy feeling her out had been an uncomfortable experience for her, this was catastrophic.

Helena's hand cautiously touched Rory's calf when neither of them spoke. "I thought I wanted everyone to be as alone as I feel." Helena shook her head. "But I don't, not really. The whole time I out, I was hoping that things would sort out between you and Michelle. Did they?"

Helena looked at Rory hopefully. Rory looked away. After several moments, she felt comfortable enough in the silence and Helena's company to close her eyes, just silently thankful that Helena was kind enough not to ask her anything else.

Chapter Thirteen

"I'm… just gonna give you guys some space," Helena said. She'd driven back from the restaurant with them, in the backseat of Michelle's car. She hadn't said a word until now. Then, in an even smaller voice, she added, "I'll be… out."

Michelle and Rory were silent for several minutes after Helena closed the door softly behind her.

Rory didn't know how to begin. She was scared that, if one of them didn't say something soon, both of them would be stuck in this silence until Helena came back.

"Okay," Michelle said finally, and Rory felt giddy with relief. At least until her next words. "I don't want to hear it from a disgruntled ex… or…" Michelle shook her head and met gazes with Rory, "whatever Tally is. I want to hear things in your words."

Having said her piece, she sat down on Rory computer chair with the air of someone who was done with speaking, at least until her request was met.

Rory took a couple of backward steps until her legs hit the side of the bed. She collapsed onto the mattress weakly. "Okay." There were two things that Michelle had asked her, and Rory wanted to address them both. "Tally's not my ex. She's not *my* anything."

Rory's hands were shaking. She pressed them against the mattress beside her thighs and pretended not to notice them; was keenly aware that Michelle's sharp eyes missed so very little.

"She's right, though." And here Rory faltered. She hadn't been ready to tell Michelle yet, but the situation had forced her into it. She had not choice but to respond to Tally's accusations now. So she forced herself not to shy away from it. "I'm afraid to drink."

Rory closed her eyes and opened them again before the fear and angst of what she was saying overwhelmed her and sealed her lips.

"So that's the big secret I've been keeping from everyone. In between uni and seeing you, I've been going to meetings. I've been telling total strangers my fears in the hope that they'll be able to fix me." Once she started, she continued almost by rote, saying the same words that she'd said to Smithy over a week before. She found that it was harder to meet Michelle's eyes. It wasn't easier having already had this conversation with Smithy. She had so much more to lose with Michelle.

She dared a glance at her girlfriend. Her face was impassive. Rory didn't know how to read it without her fears intruding.

Michelle waited patiently.

"I was ashamed. That's why I didn't tell you.

And being with you has been so much fun! I didn't want to do or say anything that might make that end. I may have kissed Tally when we were both drunk, but I—"

Rory cut herself off, reframed what she'd been about to say, and tried again.

"It is different with you. And new for me. I've never had anything like this. That's why I told you that you were the first woman I kissed. You *were* the first woman I kissed when I was fully aware of making that decision." A pleading note had entered Rory's voice. She didn't like it, but she so desperately wanted Michelle to understand; was so desperately worried that she wouldn't. "I hardly remember anything that happened with Tally, I was so drunk. And I'm ashamed of that. So I kept things from you. And that was stupid."

"It was."

Like Smithy, Michelle didn't merely mouth whatever she thought Rory wanted to hear. Rory tried to take hope in that; like they were still able to talk honestly to each other and it was still worth it to try.

"Because you kept this from me, I took you to a party where there was alcohol," Michelle continued, from between thin lips. Her voice was cool, disappointed. "Where you drank alcohol."

"And then you stopped me from drinking more," Rory reminded her, before adding in a mumble, "I thought you knew about it then."

Michelle shook her head with a foul bark of

laughter; possibly the most indelicate sound Rory had ever heard from her. "I had been drinking and I was stupid enough to forget myself and engage in a power play even though I hadn't talked it over with you first."

"We talked about that."

"Oh, I know. Thank god you didn't mind. But this…" Michelle shook her head. "I thought you trusted me."

"I do," Rory said. Then again with more feeling, "I *do* trust you."

Michelle looked at Rory silently. The words were in the air between them. *If you trusted me, why didn't you tell me this?*

Thank god she didn't actually say them out loud.

"I need to think about what you keeping this quiet means to me. I don't want to abandon you. But I need some… time," Michelle said with finality.

"Time," Rory echoed numbly.

Michelle nodded, as though hearing Rory say it strengthened her resolve. But when she looked at Rory, and really saw her again, her face did soften.

"You're dealing with a very difficult thing, and I trust that you've been battling with it the best way you know how. This isn't goodbye," Michelle told Rory forcefully, putting her hand against Rory's cheek and making sure she didn't shy away as she so desperately wanted to. "You've had longer to think about this than I have. I'm just asking for a day or two to process."

Rory just nodded her head, not trusting herself to speak yet.

Michelle's dark lashes lowered over her eyes for a moment then in one, two, three strides, Michelle held Rory in her arms, and was lifting her chin to find and kiss her lips.

Rory grasped to Michelle as though she was in very real danger of sinking, but Michelle only allowed them that small goodbye kiss before she pulled away and strode to the door, opening and then shutting it quietly behind her.

In her absence, Rory felt all the air deflate from her. This wasn't how the night was supposed to have gone. This wasn't how any of it was supposed to have gone.

~~*

Helena knocked so lightly on Rory's door when she came back that Rory almost didn't hear. She looked up when Helena pushed open the door ever so slightly.

"Is it safe to come in?" she asked quietly.

Rory remained curled up on her bed, not looking at anything.

"She's not here," she told Helena dully.

Helena came into the room and closed the door behind her just as gently as Michelle had. Rory had no idea how much time had lapsed since

Michelle left. She didn't move as the end of the bed dipped and Helena sat there. She didn't have the heart to have the same conversation with her housemate that she'd had with Michelle, even though both girls had heard what Tally had had to say that night.

Rory would have killed to have a drink right then. Several drinks. A whole bottle of scotch didn't even seem outlandish. If Smithy feeling her out had been an uncomfortable experience for her, this was catastrophic.

Helena's hand cautiously touched Rory's calf when neither of them spoke. "I thought I wanted everyone to be as alone as I feel." Helena shook her head. "But I don't, not really. The whole time I out, I was hoping that things would sort out between you and Michelle. Did they?"

Helena looked at Rory hopefully. Rory looked away. After several moments, she felt comfortable enough in the silence and Helena's company to close her eyes, just silently thankful that Helena was kind enough not to ask her anything else.

Chapter Fourteen

When Rory woke up again, it was the middle of When Rory woke up again, it was the middle of the night. Her room was dark; Helena had turned off the lights before she left the room. Rory felt cold, even though there was a blanket unfolded up to her neck. Rory found it bitterly kind of Helena to have tucked her in.

Taking one arm out from under the blanket, she reached for her mobile. There were so many texts. One from Brian. Five from Smithy. One from Michelle saying she'd gotten home all right.

Nothing else. So maybe this was why the group suggested no new relationships within a year of getting sober. But, now that things had started with Michelle, she couldn't very well stop them. Especially since Michelle had been so explicit in saying things weren't over between them. It wouldn't be fair. To Michelle, or to her.

Rory turned her phone off and laid it face down on the bedside table. Maybe it was time for her to seriously think about getting a sponsor.

The next four hours were hell spent lying in her bed, staring at the ceiling and unable to sleep. When the morning birds started their chorus, Rory's body started to relax in relief. At least daytime places would be starting to open soon. More importantly: the bars would be closed.

She still wore her clothes from the day before and didn't bother getting changed. With careful, slow movements, Rory got herself out of bed and felt around for books and her bag to take to the campus library, as going to Kismet threatened to remind her far too much of Michelle.

The morning birds were her only company as Rory trudged her and her backpack down the street that would take her to the bus that would take her to the nearest library. The grey morning echoed her mood. As she walked, a thin smattering of rain displayed the layer of mist around her.

She waited for fifteen minutes at the bus stop, grateful for the shelter, though it didn't do a great deal towards shielding her from the wind. She hadn't put on enough clothes for this. She realised this around the time that she started shivering uncontrollably about ten minutes before the bus arrived.

And then the heat. Rory almost sighed out loud as she validated her ticket and found a seat. As she looked around at the number of people in scarves and gloves, holding takeaway cups of coffee, Rory berated herself for not going across the road and buying herself a Maccas coffee. Not only might it have pulled her out of her fog of unreality, but it would have warmed the frozen blocks that had previously been her hands.

Rory shivered in her seat and incredibly aware that her toes and fingers were numb.

It took her longer than usual to pull out her phone to see if were any more messages from Michelle. Nothing, not since the *Home safe,* message from the night before. She sighed again. One or two days, Michelle had asked for. A reasonable amount of time. Since it wasn't yet ten o'clock in the morning of day one, that meant she had up to 40 hours left to wait.

Nothing difficult there.

Her phone lit up with a new message as she held it, and Rory scrambled with stiff, frozen fingers to unlock it.

But it was Helena, *Just woke up and saw you weren't home. R U OK?*

Rory considered not replying, like she'd done with Smithy, like she'd also done with Brian. But she lived with Helena. Somehow, it seemed different to not go home or reply to Helena.

She typed out a quick text with her thumbs. *On the bus.*

When the next message came through from Helena, Rory managed not to jump on it. This time, she knew it would be Helena instead of Michelle.

:) I'm going for breakfast. Wanna come?

Rory shook her head, and started writing back a 'no thanks' reply. But it wasn't exactly like the library was a better offer. All it promised that she'd be alone in a different location. Now that

Helena was awake, Rory wasn't so sure that being alone right now was the best idea for her. Blindly, she backspaced through the text that she'd written.

That'd be great. Just let me get back home.

She got off at the next stop, hardly paying attention to where she was, just walking across the road and waiting for the bus coming in the opposite direction. Thankfully, the wait for this one was less than fifteen minutes. In ten minutes, she was making the short walk back from her nearby bus stop to her place again.

Rory flipped the phone over and over in her hand as she walked, knowing that her mum was still waiting a call to confirm them catching up during the week. She genuinely tried to will herself to make it. Her mum wouldn't even have started her weekend shift yet. And, even if Daphne did miss the call, she'd be grateful for a voice message if Rory left one.

And yet, by the time Rory walked into the living room she shared with Helena, she still hadn't made the call. She slipped her phone back into her pocket before wandering into Helena's room.

Helena was standing in front of the half body height mirror in her room, touching strands of her hair and gelling them in place just so. Her eyes caught sight of Rory in the mirror and she turned around. "Where did you go? It looks frigidly cold outside."

"I couldn't sleep," Rory shrugged it off. She moved further into the room and sat on Helena's bed while she finished getting ready. "Where were you thinking of for breakfast? I can drive us so we don't both freeze." It was a viable concern. Her fingers and toes still hadn't regained feeling from her walk back from the bus stop.

Helena didn't answer until she'd finished putting earrings in, then she turned to Rory and said, "Will there still be room for a booking at that scones place you like if we call them now?"

"Let's find out," Rory said, pulling out her phone. Still no text message from Michelle.

She made a booking for the two of them, then grabbed her keys.

While they waited for their order to arrive, Rory kept waiting for more questions about where she'd been and why.

The scones were cooked on premises so, by the time they came out, it had been thirty minutes sitting there engaging in nothing more scintillating than small talk. When it seemed like that was simply going to continue, just around scones, Rory put her hand up and said, "Tally laid everything out there last night. You vacated the house so that Michelle and I could have a talk. And now you don't have any questions at all?"

Helena gave a small shrug. "It's none of my business," she said, ducking her chin in towards her chest. Then she added, "I figured you'd talk to me about it if you wanted to."

Helena was right. Rory would have. Which, apparently, was exactly what she was doing. Turned out her housemate was astute enough to just let it happen.

"I don't know where to start," Rory complained.

Helena cracked a smile at that. "If you don't know where to start, I certainly don't," she said.

The light-hearted comment made Rory smile too. "Okay." She said that a lot when it came to explanation. This conversation was starting to feel very repetitive. She started imagining having it with every person in her life, but that only made her crave a drink again to make the feeling go away.

"How about at the start," Helena offered. "What started it?"

Rory remembered waking up in bed with someone she didn't remember. After that, it all poured out, softer than it would have been if they'd been in their living room, or out in a park somewhere.

People walked in and out past them in the pursuit of breakfast. Helena's expression ranged from concerned to open to sympathetic in the space of those minutes. Rory was surprised by how much easier again the sharing was.

She took a deep breath as she finished and sat back against her chair.

"Wow," Helena said. "Well, I feel like a terrible housemate."

Rory stared at Helena, stunned. "You... what?"

"I had no idea any of this was going on!" Helena told her. "Oh, I knew something had happened with you and Tally. I thought you'd slept with her boyfriend, actually. What was his name? Smithy."

Rory just stared at Helena, open-mouthed.

"This is much better than that," Helena said in conclusion.

Rory couldn't help it. It was either laugh or cry, so she just laughed.

Chapter Fifteen

Rory sat up straighter at her AA support group. She still hadn't called her mum, but the weekend had been eventful enough. She could afford to wait for things to calm down a little bit before going ahead and having the conversation about her problem yet again. She'd sent a text to Daphne to that effect, apologising that she couldn't make it this week after all, but would Wednesday of the following week suit?

When the group came to a natural lull, she said, "I spoke to my friends about what's been going on with me over the weekend, and early this weekend." It felt different coming here this time. She wasn't here to hide from the rest of her life anymore.

Her gaze met Jason's across the room. As usual, he hadn't had anything to say so far in group, but he had a reassuring smile when she looked his way.

"I feel less like I'm going to make you cry this time if I ask if you've had a good week," he said at break by the coffee station. "You look like you're doing good."

"I've been better," Rory said honestly. "But I've been worse as well."

"That's good to hear."

Rory agreed. As Jason half turned, about to move into a conversation with a different person, Rory added, "I wanted to ask you something."

Jason raised his eyebrows in inquiry. "Shoot," he said.

"Okay. I don't know how to do this. I've never really asked anything like this before…" Rory had come here planning this tonight, but now it was the moment and her mouth felt dry and her brow felt damp.

Jason's dimple made an appearance. "I promise I won't laugh at you, whatever it is."

Rory hoped as much, but his dimple wasn't really making him the most reliable narrator.

"I was wondering how to ask someone to be a sponsor," Rory said in a rush. "*My* sponsor," she clarified, in case that hadn't been obvious.

"See, that wasn't so hard," Jason said, but at least he wasn't laughing at her. "Okay, it's really informally done. Most people just go up and ask someone they think might be compatible. There are a couple of suggestions, like: a sponsor should probably have been sober for a year or more—and see that as a good thing!—and usually it's a good idea for men to sponsor men and women to sponsor women, but since you're dating a girl, I don't suppose that'll be such a big thing. But, yeah, if they're willing to sponsor you, you're good to go."

Rory sucked her bottom lip in between her teeth. "Would you be?" she asked, below the volume of people in the kitchen. Jason leaned in closer to hear her, never close enough to actually make contact. "I mean, you seem to have been sober for a while now. Would you be willing to be a sponsor?"

She didn't think he was likely to already be a sponsor to someone here, based on the conversations they'd had before. He wanted to learn from others, not the other way around. But maybe with the closeness in their ages... Plus, there was something in learning through teaching—or sponsoring—someone else, and maybe that was a way she could get him to look at it.

For the minute, Jason just looked surprised. "You want me to be your sponsor?" he asked, as though he had heard her incorrectly.

"Yes?" Rory gritted her teeth and told herself to sound more sure of it. "Yes."

He did look a little bit deer-in-the-headlights, but Rory felt hopeful until he spoke.

"I think sponsors are also usually older..." he started.

Jason looked towards the balding man, Roger, his name was. Rory followed his gaze and frowned. She wanted someone she could relate with. Roger seemed nice enough, but he was always so quick to reframe things into his own experience.

"Oh," she said, still looking aside from Jason. "You didn't say that before."

"I didn't think…" Their gazes met again, and Jason shook his head. "I mean, what am I saying? Of course, I'm happy be your sponsor."

"You don't have to," Rory was quick to say, in case he felt obligated against his will.

"No! You just caught me by surprise. I've never been someone's sponsor before."

"Well, you're doing a really good job of it so far," Rory said, quipping for once.

"Well, I just wanna do good by you, you know," Jason said sagely.

"Ah. That's... that's quite apparent," Rory deadpanned.

Jason opened his mouth and then closed it again. "Oh," he said. "You're good."

Rory gave a small but game smile. "So how does this go from here?"

"Well, you give me your number, and I give you mine. I'm available for you to call whenever you're having a problem. I encourage you to come to the groups, which you already do; introduce you to the other members, many of which you already know; explain to you about the program…"

"I see why you were so worried about taking on a heavy responsibility," Rory said, taking out her phone and keying in his name.

"We like to curb the sarcasm of the new sponsee," Jason added.

Rory raised her eyebrows, both at the made up word, and the sentiment. "Sponsee?"

"I feel like the word has a good ring to it."

"So I can really call you any time, any day, any night?" Rory asked, as she showed him her number.

"Yeah... I suppose I'm going to have to turn my phone off silent now," Jason mused.

"Might be an idea."

They were called back into the main room for the second half of the session. Rory put her phone away until the end of the group.

When there was still no message from Michelle after she got home, Rory raised her chin. Potentially as many 26 hours to go till then. But that was okay, Rory told herself. She didn't want to rely on her girlfriend for her sobriety or wellbeing. She had a sponsor now.

And while she was still feeling strong, she flicked through Smithy's text messages. There'd been another one that afternoon, bringing the total up to six. She began to read through them from the start.

Oh my god, You have every reason to hate me, to never talk to me again. But I swear I didn't know she'd been in my phone.

I feel awful.

I dropped her home tonight, she's not here. Please call me.

Ok, duh, I'm the idiot, you're probably with your girlfriend right now trying to sort out this mess, aren't you? I'm an asshole, I'm a total asshole, but I'm a worried asshole. So when you get a minute, message me back, ok?

Are you even still talking to me?

Ok, it's probably stalkery-harassment at this point, but please. Just one message. Let me know you're ok? Please?

Rory keyed in a quick text to alleviate his guilt. *I'm okay.*

She didn't know what else she wanted to say, so she just clicked SEND.

While she thought about it, she went to reply to the text message from Brian. No sooner had she sent that message, then Smithy's first reply came back.

Ok. Thank you for replying. And then another message from him, only half a minute later: *Tally hasn't been around since last night. I don't think she's going to be again.*

Rory started to type in a reply, then refrained from asking whether that meant Smithy and Tally were no longer dating. It was none of her business.

It's fucked that she read those messages, she wrote.

I know. I'm not going to excuse it. It'll never happen again.

Despite herself, Rory wanted to believe him. And wasn't like Tally could do any worse. She'd already done all the damage she could do.

You up to anything today?

Lazing around the house, enjoying the freedom of holidays, Rory answered.

I don't suppose you… want to meet up?

Rory took her time replying to that one.

Why? she finally sent back, delaying so she could have more time to think.

She felt awful for not considering the way that would come across several seconds later when his own reply came back to her. *Because... we're friends?*

And then, *Aren't we?*

Again the two messages from Smithy came through in quick succession. Rory clicked a slow reply.

Where did you want to meet?

~~*

They organised a place to meet. Rory was late, having dragged her feet and changed her mind multiple times on the way to getting there. There were tables outside for smokers but, not being a smoker, it was far too cold for Rory to consider sitting outside. She barely gave them a passing glance as she pushed open the door and made her way into the much-vaunted central heating. As soon as she walked into the coffee place, Smithy stood up. He'd clearly been watching the door from his table.

Taking a deep breath in, Rory made her unhurried way across to him.

"I'm glad you came," he said, genuinely sounding like he meant it. Smithy didn't go so far as to reach out to hug her, though, and Rory didn't move to initiate contact either.

He sat down right after she did.

Rory tried not to feel betrayed by him. But it was difficult not to look at him different from the way she had before. So she just gave him a sad smile.

"Thank you," she said. "For everything you've done for me. I really appreciate it."

"Rory…"

"No, I do. It's important to say. I don't hold against you what happened with Tally."

"Rory, please, why don't we order coffee?" There was an uncomfortable tone to Smithy's words, a hunch to his shoulders, a twist of his mouth.

Rory just shook her head. "I don't think we're going to be here long enough for that. I just wanted to say, I don't hold it against you… But I can't get past it either. I want to—"

"We could give it some time. Tally and I have broken up."

Rory winced at his admission.

"I know that I have to earn your trust back after what happened." Smithy ducked his head until she had no choice but to look up into his eyes. "I'm willing to. You're a good friend. You're the kind of friend I'd like to keep, if that's still possible."

"I'm… not sure." Rory tried to soften the statement as much as she could, but there was no kind way to say it. "I've got to concentrate on getting myself better. It's too much trying to work on trust issues with you on top of that. You have been a good friend to me. And I appreciate it. Really. But I have to concentrate... on me right now."

She did him the courtesy of meeting his eyes as she said all of this, much as she wanted to bow her head and direct all her words to the table. As selfish as she knew it sounded, she also knew it was the right choice to make for her right now. With or without Tally, Smithy was still part of the life that she needed to leave behind.

It wasn't easy to look into the slack disappointment on Smithy's face and hold to her conviction.

"I understand." The slackness morphed into tightness across his jaw as he formed the words. His tone of voice said the very opposite.

"I'm sorry," Rory said.

Smithy just nodded, pushed his chair back, stood up, and left the coffee shop without looking back.

The coffee shop waiter finally stepped out. "So... Coffee for..." He glanced off in the direction Smithy had gone, and hazarded a guess. "Two?"

"Um, just one coffee, please," she said, hardly looking him in the eye. Coffee was a good idea. It wasn't great for her to just go wandering while she felt like this. Ideally, coffee would settle her. She focused on that hope, even as the waiter disappeared, not waiting long enough to ask her how she'd like her coffee served.

A moment later, a waitress—older and seeming more able to handle the problem customer out the front—pulled out the chair Smithy had sat in across from her.

"How would you like your coffee, sweetheart?" she asked gently.

Rory blinked rapidly, then concentrated on keeping her eyes wide to stop the tears. Even worse than the inept waiter, who was now staring at her from behind the coffee machine, was this kindly waitress looking at her with sympathetic eyes.

"Just a cappuccino, please," she said, staring at the table between them.

"Coming right up," the waitress said. She stood up and pushed the chair back in towards the table. "You're gonna be all right."

Rory caught her breath, but the waitress only offered one more sympathetic smile before heading in to make her order.

She would be okay, she told herself, strangely reassured by the kind stranger's words. But that didn't make her any less regretful for her words to Smithy. Just the thought of him, his friendship, his kindness that she'd prohibited herself from getting from him from now on. In his absence, and her own regret, she came dangerously close to forgetting all the good reasons she'd made the decision with him that she had.

When the cappuccino came out to her—delivered by the kind waitress who briefly checked in with her again—Rory took a couple of sips of it before deciding she didn't want the rest of it after all.

Paying for it, Rory went back to the refuge of her home.

It was Helena's last night at home before she headed up to her parents in Gippsland for the rest of the semester break. Helena was reading on the living room couch with the lamp dimly lighting the room when Rory came back in.

"Looking forward to seeing your parents?" Rory asked, picking up a book with the vague intent of reading.

"It's gonna be good. My sister's coming home for a couple of days during the week and bringing my new nephew. I've hardly gotten to see him so far this year." Helena laid her book on her lap and gave Rory her attention. "How about you?"

"Oh, I'll be... all right," Rory said, echoing the waitress' words. They'd sounded more convincing when the waitress had said them.

Helena accepted the words at face value. "No word yet from Michelle?" she asked.

"None." Then, because she didn't want Helena to worry if she didn't hear from Michelle before Helena went to Gippsland, "But I've got a sponsor now."

Helena looked blankly at Rory, even going so far as to mouth the word, as if that would cause it to make more sense.

"From AA. To help keep me sober," Rory

added quietly.

"Oh! Oh, well, that's fantastic!" Helena said, covering her momentary lack of understanding with effusiveness.

Rory snorted a laugh. "What time do you have to get up to leave tomorrow?"

Chapter Sixteen

Looking at her phone wasn't the first thing Rory did when she woke up but, when she did, there still weren't any messages from Michelle. These were the slowest two days she could remember in recorded history, and they still weren't over yet.

None from Smithy either, though she hadn't expected one.

There was one message from Jason. *Just making sure I've got your number right.*

Rory replied with a quick affirmative and left it at that.

Helena was already gone. Rory remembered waking briefly at some point in the early hours while her housemate got dressed and grabbed the things she'd left near the door. Then Rory had fallen back to sleep. Now she walked across the empty living room, staying there for about ten minutes before she realised she wanted somewhere that had more people.

The campus was quiet over the semester break, but she knew the subjects she had coming up. It couldn't hurt to do a bit of preparatory reading ahead of time.

Rory cut across the nearly empty car park at

the back of the on campus housing swaddled in her jacket over the jumper, scarf and fingerless gloves. She was surprised when someone called out her name.

"Hey, Aurora."

The guy looked vaguely familiar, so Rory turned around and took a couple of steps towards the guy who had paused in the middle of packing stuff into the back of his car.

"That was your name, right? Aurora?" the guy added when Rory looked at him blankly.

"Hey." Rory couldn't say his name. She didn't remember it. She was surprised he remembered hers. The greeting fell away and her hand dropped to her side. "Thought nobody would be here," she murmured.

"Nah, parties last night. There's a few of us heading up to Wilson's Prom today."

Rory waited, ready to refuse the invitation she thought she saw coming, but the moment passed without invite.

"That sounds nice," Rory said, trying to sound interested as she also tried to remember where she knew him from.

The guy nodded as he pushed down his boot with a *clunk*. "Hey, look, I was a dick last time we met. I was hungover, and you…" He shrugged, as though what she'd done to cause his being a dick should have been self-explanatory.

Rory nodded along with him before the reference he was making struck home.

"Oh," she uttered, before she could stop herself. She took an involuntary step back. Her lips suddenly couldn't form another word.

"Yeah, well, I figure it's fine. Water over the bridge months ago, right?" Matt waved a hand in the air as if to make nothing of the whole thing.

She couldn't stop staring at him, and yet she wasn't seeing him. She was seeing a bed, where she'd waken up in bed under him, having been too drunk to make that decision herself. He'd yelled at her, and now he was implying that it was either her fault or maybe hardly important enough to mention at all.

Rory blinked several times, trying to get the sudden vivid flashback from replaying over and over in her mind's eye.

"Hey, are you okay?" He didn't advance towards her, but scrunched up his face as though she'd done something that was unappealing to him.

Rory would have wondered if she'd flushed white or red. She hadn't expected to see Matt again, certainly not all these months later. Maybe what he was looking at was the pulse point in her throat fluttering desperately as if trying to shoot its way free of the skin.

She shook her head, feeling the blonde ends of her hair whipping her face in her vehemence. "No, I'm all right," she said.

The reassurance wasn't for him. It was for her, but she didn't believe it.

"All right…" Matt didn't look like he believed it either, but it was more convenient for him to make out like he did. "Well, the guys are waiting. I had better…" Again, he just gestured instead of finishing the sentence.

Rory gaped at him until he looked away, then turned and walked away as if nothing had happened.

Nothing had happened, and yet everything had happened.

Her body felt like it was shaking itself apart. She almost dropped her phone three times in her attempt to bring up Jason's number and call him. The phone rang. And rang. And rang out.

"Hello, this is Jason, you know what to do."

BEEP.

"Jason? It's Rory. From group. I'm having… I'm having a… a problem. A big one. Could you please call me back? Thanks."

She stood alone in the car park for moments before she realised that Matt and his friends would be coming back this way to pile into the car before long. She ran out of the car park, not even noticing the direction she was going beyond that. She didn't want to be alone. She didn't want to be alone right now. She glanced again at her phone as though that would magically make it start ringing, and almost tripped over before looking at the ground again.

Her feet got her out of the car park and then seemed to know where they were going of her own volition. Rory herself felt absent, hollowed out, as though seeing Matt had brought back something she'd been doing her best to bury. She told herself to breathe. Just breathe. And, when that didn't work, she told herself to drink. Just to wet the back of her throat. And maybe to help her breathe.

She was feeling so much better a couple of drinks later in the middle of the uni bar that was hosting happy hour.

~~*

Rory opened her eyes to look up at Michelle. Michelle's face wore an expression of worry, her eyes wide and eyebrows slanted down away from the bridge of her nose, but as Rory's gaze focused on her, Michelle's expression changed. Michelle evaluated her face, her body, and seemed to come up with some decision that she didn't share before she turned away.

Rory closed her eyes again. Opened them. Looked around. She was still in the same place. She had no idea how she'd ended up in Michelle's bedroom.

"Here." A glass of water came into Rory's field of vision, and she became aware of a steady pounding behind her eyes. "Drink this."

Memories were starting to come back to her.

Oh. Oh no.

"Michelle, I—!"

The glass shook, water straining at the lip of the glass, threatening to topple over. "I don't want to hear it until you've drunk this."

It was a clear enough instruction. Rory obeyed without saying anything more, lifting a hand up heavily and taking the glass.

Only once she was finished did she dare say, "How did I…?"

"A stranger answered your phone." Michelle's lips were a flat line of disapproval. There was no need to ask for more details on what had happened. Rory could imagine it all too easily.

Michelle set the empty glass upon the bedside table.

"Important question time." Michelle stared at Rory sternly from behind her glasses. To Rory, who still felt somewhat like waking up in a strange world after a too long sleep, Michelle looked more like some glorious, avenging figure out of myth than her girlfriend. "Do you want to get sober?"

Michelle's question brought Rory back down to earth with a thud. "Of *course* I want to get sober," she whispered. God, if Michelle didn't even believe that, how was Rory ever going to face her?

"Good." Michelle's tone was clipped, unaffected by Rory's emotions. "Because this is going to be hard. You may have a weakness to alcohol that other people don't have, but what's going to beat this is you. Not me. Not Helena. Not anybody else. So you see why the question's important."

Michelle was brutally efficient. Everything from her words to her footsteps across the room were clipped. She looked like she was only tenuously hanging onto her own sense of control.

"And BDSM is off the table," Michelle said. "I am not going to control this addiction for you."

Rory didn't say anything. She couldn't think of anything to say, any argument to raise.

"Okay," she said, softly, when the eyes boring into her demanded a response.

Somehow, Michelle's tough love was harsher for Rory to face than the hangover. She needed to get out of bed and go to the bathroom, but wasn't sure how to bring it up in the face of Michelle's obvious disapproval.

"I'll get you another glass of water," Michelle said, turning abruptly on her heel and leaving the bedroom.

Rory closed her eyes. Moments later, she felt the wetness of tears trailing down towards her ears. She didn't open her eyes when she heard Michelle come back into the room, but she did hear her girlfriend's gaze stop abruptly several feet away from the bed.

"I'm sorry," she uttered, feeling hopelessly shamed and inadequate.

Michelle came to sit on the bed and took one of Rory's hands in hers. "I'm scared too," she said suddenly. Her voice sounded completely different to how it'd been since Rory woke up. "I'm terrified of having another girlfriend who says I've harmed her."

"I'm still your girlfriend?" Rory asked in a very small voice.

"Of *course*, you are," Michelle said, tightening her hold on Rory hand. Then she pulled Rory to her, wrapping her into her arms until they were both holding on tightly.

"You were just so cold…" Rory didn't know how to articulate how she felt Michelle had every right to her coldness, yet how it made her feel at the same time. Instead of getting bogged down in that, she added, because it was important to them both, "You haven't harmed me. Not at all."

"I abandoned you," Michelle replied.

"You needed time to process." Rory winced as a wave of pain moved across her temples, but didn't let it distract her. "It was a reasonable request."

"What happened?" The words came out ragged, sounding naked and without any of the usual walls Michelle kept up around her.

"Last night?"

Michelle nodded.

"I saw Matt." Realising Michelle had no idea who Matt was, Rory went on. "He was… the reason that I stopped drinking." There was a heavy pause between her words. Obviously, there was more to the story than Rory was sharing, but Michelle didn't push for the rest of it.

Neither woman moved and Rory felt comforted by the physical contact between them. But...

"I think I need to get up," Rory said.

Rory certainly wasn't bedridden, but still Michelle's keen eyes watched her closely.

"Are you sure?" she asked.

"Yeah. I, uh, need to go to the bathroom."

"Ah."

~~*

Michelle took the day off work on Monday—the day Rory woke up in her bed—but she couldn't take Tuesday off as well.

"Will you be okay by yourself?" Michelle asked, her low voice serious.

"I'll be fine. I don't expect you to look after me. I'll find something else to do."

Michelle looked at Rory, but what she saw there seemed to convince her. That night, the two of them moved comfortably around each other in the kitchen. They made dinner that was shortly thereafter followed by eating dinner on the couches in front of the DVD player. Rory kept her socks on, but her feet were still cold enough that she kept searching for warmth on and around Michelle.

"My god, I've moved almost to the edge of the couch, but your feet keep following me!" Michelle grumbled.

Rory tried to look innocent of it, but knew that she failed.

"Mm," Michelle said, eyeing the offending feet.

Rory kept them under her butt until at least halfway through the movie when Michelle's guard lowered again.

When Michelle left in the morning, it was only with the insistence that Rory was to treat her home like her own. Rory sat bare foot on the couch with the sun streaming in the floor to near ceiling sliding back door. Out of habit, she picked up her phone to check for messages. There were two voicemails from Jason.

"Hey Rory. Good to hear from you. Sorry to hear you're having a problem, and also that I left my phone at home. Give me a call when you get this and we'll sort this out." Having listened to the first one, Rory went straight on to the next one. "Hey Rory, I'm a little bit worried, but also cool and calm and collected. Just calling again in case you didn't get my last message. Call me back when you get this, yeah?"

Rory called him immediately, and Jason answered on the first ring.

"Hey Rory. Been thinking of you."

Rory wondered if she heard censure in his tone, or whether she was projecting.

"You still there?"

"Yeah. Still here."

"So, I hear you had a bit of a problem the other day. Did you want to talk about it?"

"I guess I kind of have to, don't I?"

"Not at all." Jason's voice was calm and comfortable as he'd said in his voicemail. Rory started thinking that she had been projecting censure onto him. "I'm here to listen or whatever else you need. What are you up to today?"

Rory described the day in Michelle's living room, sitting with the sun warming her toes, the open air of her girlfriend's house on one of the first nice weather days they'd had since winter had begun.

"Sounds like you're really are making yourself at home," Jason said. Rory could hear the smile in his voice. "Do you have any plans to take a walk this afternoon, or something?"

Rory didn't, but she wondered if she should. "Is exercise supposed to be a good idea with alcoholism, like it is with depression?" she asked.

"Yeah, I've heard arguments for it," Jason replied. "A lot of rehabs use it as part of their programme. Something about it reducing the cravings for some people, not really sure how though."

"Well maybe I'll go for a walk later on," she said.

"Good for you!"

Rory snorted. "You're very good at this being inspiring thing, did you know? I'm imagining you with little pom poms."

Jason laughed out loud at that. "Should I be worried for the sake of my masculinity?"

"Not at all." Rory hadn't realised she'd been worried that Jason becoming her sponsor would make things more serious between them. Instead, she felt just like she was talking to a friend who understood what she was going through.

With a pang, she thought again of Smithy, and hoped he was doing well.

Without the expectation that she talk about what had happened the other day, Jason made her want to share the experience; he made it feel like it was safe to do so.

"There was this guy," Rory started. The words started heavily, and Rory felt like she was changing the mood dramatically as she opened her mouth to speak. She wished they were sitting in front of each other in person; she would have liked to see his facial expression as she told her story. "There was this guy near the start of semester. I was drunk when I ended up in bed with him. I don't remember any of it but I feel… I feel… We slept together. And I feel… It wasn't consensual. I wasn't in a state where I could have consented."

Jason was silent while she shared her experience, just like he would have been in group. Rory felt a hard lump forming in the back of her throat. Her eyes were already moist and threatening to overflow. She took in a shuddering breath.

"I feel like it's my fault. Like I had sex against my will, and it was my fault."

She couldn't focus on that fact for more than a few seconds, so she rushed onto the next statement before Jason could say anything.

"I saw him. Matt. His name's Matt. And I saw him at uni for the first time since then. That was when I called you. And then, somehow, I ended up in the university bar. I don't remember the rest. When I woke up, I was here, at Michelle's. She was freaked out about leaving me to go to work today. She'd be really glad to hear I'm talking to you."

"I'm glad she would," Jason said with feeling. "And I'm sorry you had to go through that experience."

Rory could hear him forming his words really carefully. "I don't need you to counsel me about the experience with Matt. That's…" Rory shook her head without thinking or caring that he couldn't see it. "I just don't want it to be my first response to something difficult to go and drink my way through a bar." She lost it then, and the sound of her sob travelled its way through the phone.

Jason was silent for a while. Then he said in a forcedly light tone of voice, "That's why I'm here. That's the idea of a sponsor. Together, we can do what we could not do alone!"

Rory gave a gurgling laugh through her tears. "You rolled your eyes as you said that, didn't you?"

"Totally did," Jason said sagely.

~~*

Michelle enveloped her in a close hug when she got home, murmuring into her ear, "How has your day been?" Her lower lip lingered against Rory's earlobe, causing Rory to shiver.

"Very good." Rory had found a café that, while not as nice as Kismet, still had a vaguely bohemian feel. Tea bags were in a box near the register, and patrons were encouraged to pick them up and sniff them before making their preference. She'd sat there, reading a book that she'd found on Michelle's shelves, for about an hour before coming back home.

Michelle saw it as they pulled apart. "Ah. I see you went through my bookshelves," she said, picking up the book and flipping it between her hands.

"Well, you did say to make myself at home," Rory said.

"So I did." Michelle handed the book back to Rory. "But you've picked up the second book in the series."

"I don't mind." Truthfully, at 100 pages in, she was already engaged in the story, and the important events of the previous one had already been covered.

"Do you have a favourite character?" Michelle asked silkily.

Rory looked down, then up at Michelle through her lashes. "Well, there is one character…"

Michelle raised her eyebrows in silent encouragement for Rory to continue.

Rory rolled her eyes. "Well, it's your book. You obviously know that the main character experiences pleasure and pain as the same thing."

"I do," Michelle said. Her eyes smiled and she spoke in a contented murmur.

As they went about making dinner, Rory told Michelle about her day, about her phone conversation with Jason and the walk that had followed. Michelle in turn shared the busy-ness of her day, minor irritations at work that hadn't gotten done in her absence.

"I'd like to meet him," Michelle said, over dinner.

"Who? Jason?" Rory asked.

"Who else?"

"Well, yeah… I guess we could do that. Sure."

Chapter Seventeen

Rory texted him to organise it the next time that he checked in with her to see how she was going. He was game. As it turned out, Kismet was quite close to where he lived. Michelle smiled when Rory told her that.

"Sounds like nostalgia to me."

They arranged to meet for dinner a week later. And yet, when it actually happened, it felt so strange for Rory to sit at a table with Michelle on one side of her, and Jason on the other.

"This is a nice place," Jason said, looking around them. "I can't think why I haven't come here before."

Michelle smiled her usual smile at him and held Rory's hand under the table.

"I've heard lots of great things about you," Jason said, looking back towards Michelle.

"And I about you," Michelle said, neutrally.

Dear god, the two of them were so, so different.

"Drinks?" Rory asked, then blanched. "I mean…"

"We know what you mean, love," Michelle said. "Coffee would be lovely."

"Do they do juice here?" Jason asked.

"Let's ask," said Michelle.

It was strange. When it was just Rory and Michelle, or just Rory and Jason, Rory had no problem with holding her own part of the conversation. Something about the three of them in the same room together changed the dynamic more than she could reconcile. Thankfully, the two of them seemed content to lead the conversation.

"So, Jason," said Michelle, after their round of non-alcoholic drinks had arrived. "What do you do?"

"What, you mean apart from being a recovering alcoholic?" Jason asked. He ducked his head and chuckled under his breath. "Sorry, recovery humour. It's not very funny. I'm a retail assistant."

"Oh. That must mean terrible hours," Michelle said.

"That's true. Most Thursday and Fridays are late shifts. But at least the Sunday pay is good."

Rory tuned out most of the small talk. She noted how Jason was as fair as Michelle was dark. Only their eyes were the exception. Jason's warm, brown eyes told so much about the easy going attitude he had. They gave Rory hope that she could go through something like this and come out of it still able to smile. Michelle's pale, icy blue eyes behind her dark framed glasses spoke more of the hurt she guarded herself against. Rory had to believe there was something good about her, despite her addiction, otherwise she very much believed Michelle would not still be around.

Seeing them talking to each other for the very first time, easy going and guarded respectively, was an interesting interplay to watch.

"Rory?" Jason's voice was amused, his eyes smiling, and Rory had the sense this wasn't the first time her name had been said. "Have you decided what you wanted for dinner?"

"Yeah," Rory said, smiling at Michelle. "I'll have my usual."

~~*

"I liked him," Michelle said, as they got ready for bed that night. She was in her cream nightgown. Rory had made the trip back to her house during the week to get some of her own clothes, and was wearing her own pyjamas again.

She turned the overhead light off, which sunk the bedroom into lamplight. Michelle was already in the bed, propped up against the pale pillows, blankets pooling around her waist. She pinned Rory with her sultry gaze as Rory approached.

"How well can you actually see me right now?" Rory asked, seeing Michelle's glasses in the case beside the bed. Usually she wasn't on the other side of the room when Michelle looked at her like that.

"Right now, you are an incredibly attractive blur," Michelle told her, sitting up in the bed and drawing Rory to her. "Ah, now, that's better."

Rory allowed Michelle to take her into her arms, but she kept herself on her knees, which left her taller than Michelle's seated form for once.

She draped her arms over Michelle's shoulders and kissed one of her girlfriend's temples, then the other. Michelle was gazing up at her archly when she drew to the front of her again. Without saying a word, Rory kissed first one cheek, then the other. Then the tip of Michelle's nose, watching as it crinkled, and Michelle glared up at her. Rory couldn't find it within herself to feel anything less than perky as she finally lowered her butt to the heels of her feet and kissed Michelle lightly on the lips.

Michelle's arms tightened around her, and she pressed her lips to Rory's encouraging them open gently, then more insistently, the tip of her tongue lazily dipping in and out of Rory's mouth.

Rory moaned despite herself.

"I've been thinking..." Rory said, pressing her top half against Michelle, delighting in the feeling of Michelle's fingers bunching and unbunching in the fabric at Rory's back. "About that book of yours that I borrowed."

"Hmm?" Michelle said, but Rory could tell she wasn't very interested in what Rory was saying. Her lips had already found their way to Rory's neck, and suddenly Rory was finding it very hard to stay interested in what she was saying.

"Like, the way that it's just the way she was

born, just something that's part of her. Not something she needs to be embarrassed about, or something she can change…"

Michelle lifted her head from Rory's neck as she started to realise that her girlfriend wasn't in the same place, and then tuning into the words Rory was saying. "Babe, we've talked about this," she said.

"I know. But I've been doing good."

"It's not about you doing good—" Michelle started.

"And you've met Jason now," Rory interrupted. "He's my support with this stuff. I don't want that for you. I don't want you to feel like you have to look after me."

"I don't feel like I need to look after you." Michelle sat back, leaning her back against the headboard.

"And I also want to make sure that you're getting what you need. From me. From us."

"Sweetie." Michelle looked at Rory very seriously. "I am."

Rory opened her mouth, but this time Michelle interrupted her.

"No. I need you to listen to me. It's very nice that I met Jason, and I'm happy you've got that support. None of that means I'm not still here for you myself."

"But I—"

"And being here for you doesn't mean I'm going to look at you differently. It just means I like being here for you."

Michelle's eyes flashed, warning Rory not to make an immediate argument. After several minutes of staring at each other, Rory gaze lowered to the sheets.

"Lastly," Michelle said, censure clear in her voice now. "If you want that kind of aspect in our relationship, demanding it is not the way to do it."

Rory pressed her lips together, still looking down, sufficiently chastised. "I can see how that would be."

Michelle smirked. "Now, if you're done talking…"

Rory lifted her gaze, still biting her lip. Michelle rolled her eyes, grabbed Rory, pressed her down against the mattress, and kissed her until there were no more words.

Chapter Eighteen

It was Saturday morning when Michelle made them breakfast. Rory kept having her hands swatted for trying to steal strawberries.

"Do that again and I'll cut one of them off," Michelle said, gesturing with her knife.

"Yes, ma'am." Rory pretended to look chastised which, since it was a very different look to when she felt properly chastised, was dead obvious.

"Trouble," Michelle muttered under her breath. It had become something of a pet name between them.

Instead of going for another strawberry, Rory went to use this moment between them as a sort of buffer. It hadn't worked well when Tally ambushed them, but maybe a calm, civilised conversation about it while they were feeling comfortable in Michelle's home would make it better this time.

"I have something I need to tell you," Rory said finally. "Something you should possibly know."

Michelle stopped, and put the knife down.

Rory eyes rounded. "What?"

"I know what that tone means from you," Michelle said. "I thought it might be best to put down the knife first."

"Well now, that's not fair," Rory said, considering this might not have been such a great idea after all.

Michelle just stared at her until Rory was quailed into going back to her original plan.

"All right. I wasn't comfortable talking about this before now. Erm. So at the start of the year, just after semester started, there was this party. The one where I stopped drinking. Well, the thing is, the reason is that…" Rory's words started coming faster and she was scared again that this story was going to overwhelm her like it so often did.

Michelle began to look concerned.

"Someone had sex with me," Rory said, just cutting to the chase. She couldn't look at Michelle as she said it, and would have berated herself as a coward for that if it wasn't already so hard just to utter these words. "I wasn't sober enough to give consent. It was before you and me got together, but… that's why… When I went off the rails…"

"You saw him that day," Michelle said without inflection.

Rory just nodded.

Michelle opened her mouth, then closed it, clearly choosing silence over anything else she could say.

Very slowly, she reached for the knife and went back to making breakfast for the two of them.

Shocked, Rory just watched her. "Umm…"

"I was raped." The words were shocking as they came out of nowhere. Just like Rory, Michelle didn't manage to look at her girlfriend as she said the words. "When I was 19. It was a completely different situation, but I was raped too."

Only at the end did she lift her head to meet Rory in the eye.

Shocked no longer described the way Rory felt.

Michelle looked away again. "If you want to talk to me about it, I'm someone who can understand. But I also understand if it's too painful to talk about. It must have been a very hard thing for you to tell me."

"You too…" Rory said, increasingly confounded by Michelle's ongoing dispassionate words. She didn't quite know how to respond.

"I will just say one thing." Michelle looked up at her over her glasses. "You did get yourself checked? After he…"

"It was the first thing I did," Rory said solemnly.

"And you weren't…?"

"Pregnant? Or diseased?" Rory asked.

"Both," Michelle said. Her gaze warmed a little this time as she looked at Rory. She shrugged. "Either."

"No STIs and nothing else unexpected either," Rory said.

She watched as Michelle nodded, then her

throat moved as she swallowed, looking away from Rory. "You know, the statistics are up to 1 in 5 women experiencing sexual violence in Melbourne?" Michelle shook her head as she continued to cook. It was like the action of putting their breakfast together was allowing her to talk like this. "It's beyond upsetting."

"Michelle…"

"And it's getting worse," Michelle said, her movements becoming more jerky. "Every time I watch the news, it seems like some other girl has been taken off the streets at night and raped and murdered. And those are only the ones that are televised."

"Michelle," Rory said again. She rounded the counter and approached Michelle slowly, waiting until their eyes met before she initiated physical contact. "It's okay. It's okay. I'm here, okay?"

Michelle stared at her, blinked once, then again. The knife dropped with a clatter against the bench. The first of Michelle's tears broke from beneath her high walls, and Rory was there to hold her, comfort her, be there for her.

"I'm sorry," she said, her voice sounding muffled with her face pressed against Rory's shoulder. "I'm sorry. I shouldn't be like this now. This was something to do with you. I don't want to take away from that…"

"Shh," Rory said, holding Michelle firmly. "You aren't taking away from anything. You're here for me, remember? I'm here for you too."

"Okay…" Michelle seemed to accept that. Rory knew that the tears hadn't stopped, though, from the way Michelle's shoulders heaved, and the dampness on her shoulder grew.

At some point, Michelle took her glasses off. Rory made sure they didn't fall off the counter since Michelle wasn't looking at where she put them. Rory didn't ask any questions, didn't shh her or say anything more until Michelle was cried out.

She pulled away from Rory, wiping at her eyes before reaching for her glasses again. It was a long moment before she met Rory's gaze again. "I should… I probably need to explain what happened there."

"Only if you're ready to," Rory told her, meaning it.

Michelle's gaze softened, and she reached out lightly to touch Rory's cheek with the tips of her fingers. Then she bit her lip. Her gaze drifted away from Rory's, and her hand dropped. Rory caught it in hers, wanting to still keep that piece of connection between them.

"I…" Michelle didn't look at Rory as she started to speak again, and Rory didn't try to make her. She just held Michelle's hand between both of hers and hoped that was enough to remind her that she was not alone right now. "I was pregnant."

Rory closed her eyes. Her lips mouthed a silent curse, before she opened her eyes again.

"I was pregnant," Michelle said again, her voice less of a breath the second time it came out. "It was possibly the only time I'd ever be pregnant..." She took a deep breath, abruptly pulling away from Rory. Rory let her, keeping a close eye on her. Michelle glanced at her. "I terminated the pregnancy," she said quickly, before looking away again. She shook her head quickly. "It was his— I couldn't—"

"I understand," Rory whispered. "Of course you didn't wanna have his."

Michelle nodded jerkily. She hardly even looked like her. The face that was always so animated was now stripped clear of emotion. And she was pale. So pale. Still gazing at her, Rory walked around her to pour a glass of water from the sink. She held it out to Michelle wordlessly.

"Thanks," Michelle murmured, her lips barely moving. "It was such a hard decision," she whispered into the glass, before taking a sip.

Rory nodded. She didn't know what to say. What was there to say?

For several moments, the two of them stood silently in the kitchen, breakfast completely forgotten. Michelle finished the glass of water and put in on the bench beside them. Another moment passed, and then Michelle reached out for Rory's hands. She gave them freely. And then Michelle pulled her into a hug. It was clumsy, but Rory barely noticed. Her fingers were too busy stroking over Michelle's hair and arms. If physical contact was a comfort to her right now, that was exactly what she deserved.

When Michelle finally pulled away from her, there was colour in her face again. Rory was glad to see it. She reached out to wipe away a stray tear that Michelle didn't look like she noticed. "Thank you," Michelle murmured.

"For what?" Rory didn't think Michelle was thanking her for wiping her tear.

"For making it so easy to tell you that. I've only told the girls. Steve, Katrina, Gemma. It's something that's too hard to share with anyone else."

Rory understood that deeply. "I'm glad you could share it with me."

"Did you want to... tell me what happened with you?" Michelle offered a small smile. "I promise I won't fall apart on you again."

Rory smiled at her indulgently. "You don't have to make that sort of promise. For me, it was just the act. Nothing afterwards. There's not a lot more than what I told you. Seeing him again..." Rory shook her head. "He made me feel like it was my fault. I know it's not."

"It's not," Michelle reinforced.

"For either of us," Rory said. She stepped closer to Michelle again. "May I kiss you right now?"

"Please," Michelle said.

~~*

Rory kissed Michelle's temple later that afternoon. Their bodies were turned in towards each other on the bed, legs intertwined, Michelle's face pressed against the side of her neck. After the onslaught of emotion that morning, both girls had made the decision to let the rest of the day move on without going back to distressing topics. The curtains had been pushed open when they'd first gotten out of bed, so the sunlight streamed into the room, warming them without the cooling wind that swayed the trees outside.

"Oh, I see why you do this," Rory said, her fingers returning again to Michelle's part and stroking down. Her fingers trailed through hair that was long enough to fall over her bare shoulder and arm and Michelle snuggled in closer.

"It's soothing, isn't it?" she murmured.

"Very."

"Welcome to a little bit of insight on what it's like to be me."

"You like holding people in bed and stroking their hair?" Rory asked, raising her eyebrows archly. "I'll have to keep that in mind and try not to get jealous."

"Stroking their hair, yes. It's generally agreed to be a pleasant experience. I like to give people that."

"You're a giver," Rory said. "Must be why all your friends think so highly of you."

"I thought so."

Michelle's arms tightened around her, and Rory felt but didn't say how she liked looking after her so often stronger girlfriend. She rested her chin against the top of Michelle's head. She thought about the strength that Michelle wrapped around herself. She wondered whether Michelle had always seemed so strong, or whether it was something that had happened as a reaction to the rape. It was something she would never ask.

"I need to pee," Michelle grumbled, "but I don't want to move. Could you go for me?"

"Sure," Rory said, feigning getting up from the bed.

Michelle held tighter as soon as she started to move. "No, that isn't going to work either. You're the best part of the hug."

"You're biased," Rory said.

"Yes, but I'm the best part of the bias," came the reply.

Rory rolled her eyes, feeling secretly happier than she remembered feeling in a long time.

Her stomach grumbled. Rory did her best to ignore it, her best not to remind Michelle that they hadn't eaten since breakfast. But Michelle wasn't slow, wasn't too easily distracted.

"All right," she said, still not moving her head from Rory's neck and collarbone. "New plan: I'll get up and go to the toilet if you go to the kitchen and steal more than strawberries."

"That's probably a better idea than me going to

the toilet for you," Rory said, but she didn't move either.

Moments passed.

"Okay, one of us need to move here," Michelle said.

"I vote it should be you," Rory said.

"What's your reasoning?"

"You're lying on one of my arms," Rory came back.

"Ah, but one of *your* arms is on top of me."

With a grunt and a disproportionally weighted movement, Rory threw the top arm onto the mattress behind her. Michelle responded by pushing her face closer into Rory neck.

"Okay, I'm getting up," Michelle said, untwining her legs first and removing her head and torso from Rory and the bed last.

Rory sat up and curled her arms around her upraised knee as Michelle walked around the bed, towards the bathroom. She knew her hair was hopelessly tousled, was aware she was giving her girlfriend unashamed bedroom eyes, and didn't even blush when Michelle looked away and reaffirmed pointedly that she was heading to the toilet rather than back to bed.

Only after Michelle had vanished into the en suite and closed the door behind her did Rory push herself off the bed and start making the batter in the kitchen into pancakes.

~~*

On Tuesday night, Rory began to mentally prepare herself for going over to her mum's place the following night. Michelle moved to put her arms around Rory, but Rory stepped out of the way with a quick shake of her head.

"Babe?" Michelle asked, lowering her chin and looking worried.

Rory shook her head, then worked up words to her mouth when Michelle only raised an eyebrow at her. "My mum," she answered. "I'm going to see her tomorrow night. I'm finally going to tell her what's been going on."

Michelle's hand went back to her side. She looked torn as she stood there on the pot, just watching Rory.

"Would you... would you like me to come with you?"

"Would you?"

Michelle looked at her as though she was an idiot. Rory supposed she was, a bit.

Daphne lived on a wide suburban street, green grass in front of every house and no sign of recent development lots. No townhouses for a couple of blocks, and every house in the street looked like it had been there for at least twenty years. Daphne's house was one of the few that looked at least like it had had a recent coat of paint. Daphne loved painting. The inside of her house changed colour yearly as different colours came in and out of fashion.

The front garden was a wild mass of different colours and flowers. Ferns rose up against the fence. A single lemon tree grew in the middle of the yard and not a blade of grass, not a single weed, grew until the nature strip. Daphne spent most of her free time in this garden. It was her pride and joy.

Rory and Michelle stepped out of Michelle's car on Wednesday to find Daphne in the front yard gardening. She had a smudge of dirt over her right eyebrow and gloves that were absolutely covered in filth. It was the first day of the year that had actually felt like spring, and the garden smelled like it. The sun had just begun to set, so Rory didn't feel like she was pulling her mum out of her gardening too early.

"Hey Mum," Rory called, in case Daphne hadn't heard the car pulling up.

"Rory!" Daphne stood up, opened her arms and took Rory in for a long hug. She smelled of dirt and the shampoo she used. Rory could feel tears pricking at the backs of her eyelids and pushed them back.

"Mum," she said, pulling away slowly, "there's someone I'd like you to meet."

Daphne looked over Rory's shoulder to see Michelle. Her eyebrows rose. "So I see." She held her hand out, pulled it back, took off the glove and extended it again a second time. "I'm Daphne."

"I know," Michelle replied. "Rory speaks about you a lot. I'm Michelle."

Daphne grinned broadly, then she said, "Well this calls for a glass of wine. What are we doing all standing out here?" She took the other gardening glove off, and they all walked towards the porch. Daphne left the gloves on the table there and led them inside.

Rory saw Michelle look at her, but she wasn't going to make a comment about it, not while they were outside where any of the neighbours could look out of their windows and see.

Books on decorating and gardening covered the coffee table inside. Daphne actually read them and used them for inspiration, rather than buying just for something pretty to look at or inspire conversation.

Daphne never had difficulty inspiring conversation. As eclectic as her front yard, her house boasted decades of collectables from various flea markets, hand-me-downs and presents. Although she didn't regularly throw anything out, her home wasn't cluttered. Everything had a place, her mum had told her often while Rory was growing up, mostly when Rory's belongings became splayed all across her room and the living room.

Rory tried to see her mum's house from Michelle's for the first time, and couldn't. It was impossible to quantify the shelves that lined both sides of the hallway, just above head height, and held everything from porcelain dolls to babushkas. It was difficult at a glance to separate the bottles of alcohol that were for drinking from what was for show. Daphne had travelled extensively in her youth and had Rory quite late. She said she liked to have at least one bottle for each place she'd visited.

Rory suddenly realised what a terrible house this would be for her to come back to if her mum ever asked her to house sit.

"What can I get for you?" Daphne asked Michelle, pulling a bottle of chardonnay out of the fridge and half turning to Rory's girlfriend.

"Uh, actually…" Rory started, before Michelle could answer. Michelle's shoulders immediately appeared a lot less tense. She swore she saw her girlfriend exhale in relief.

Her mum's eyes turned to her.

"About the wine…" Rory said. This sentence was already taking forever to get out.

"Yes?" Daphne asked curiously. There was no sign on her face of what Rory was about to say to her. Why should there be, Rory wondered self-deprecatingly. She'd done such a good job of keeping it from her over the past several months.

"I was thinking of having orange juice," Rory said in a rush.

"Well that's fine," Daphne said, still with an easy smile on her lips. "How about you, Michelle? Would you prefer orange juice to wine?"

"Yes, please," Michelle said, sending a look towards Rory.

Rory broke eye contact and stared at the off

white linoleum floor as if wishing it could have this conversation with her mum instead of her. "Actually, that's not all I need to tell you," Rory said quietly. "Um, you might want to sit down for this."

There were two bar chairs against the kitchen bench. Slowly reaching out for one, Daphne pulled it out and sat down, looking between Michelle and Rory. "Okay, darling, you're making me a little bit worried right now," she said.

"You don't need to be worried," Rory said quickly. "You're probably going to be anyway, but I have it under control. I have been going to meetings. Mum… I have a drinking problem."

And after all that, after all of the putting it off and not being able to talk about it, it was almost easy to have the words out between them.

"Oh." Daphne put the bottle down. She looked at it, as if only just realising what she'd been holding, then her hand let go of it as if it hurt her. Again, she looked at Rory. "Oh sweetheart."

"I didn't want to worry you," Rory said, realising now that her mum would never have been disappointed in her. She would only be disappointed in Rory if she realised she had thought that. So Rory kept those pointless fears to herself.

"And you've been dealing with this on your own?" Daphne said, gaze flickering towards Michelle.

"Not alone," Rory said. "Not completely. There

was a long time there that I didn't want to admit to anyone what was going on. But I've got a sponsor now. I'm ready to be honest about this."

Daphne got up from the bar chair and crossed the kitchen to wrap her daughter up in her arms. It was a longer hug this time, one Rory didn't attempt to cut short.

When they finally pulled away from each other, Rory looked towards Michelle and saw that her eyes were glassy before she blinked a couple of times and forced a smile from behind her glasses.

"Come here," she said, lifting her arm and drawing Michelle in.

Quietly, behind them, Daphne set the bottle of chardonnay back in the fridge and pulled out the orange juice for all of them to share.

~~*

The night went perfectly. Daphne loved Michelle, and Rory was pretty sure the feeling was mutual.

They said their goodbyes around nine p.m. with acknowledgement to the fact that both Daphne and Michelle had early starts the next day.

"So, that was your mum," Michelle said, clicking her seat belt into place and starting the car before she looked at Rory.

"That's her," Rory said with a smile carrying

over from the pleasant night. She honestly couldn't have hoped for it to have gone better.

"You did really well." Michelle said it seriously. The car purred, but Michelle hadn't taken it out of neutral yet. "I'm proud of you."

"I didn't do it for that reason," Rory said. "I—"

"I know," Michelle said, interrupting her. "You didn't."

Rory didn't know what to say to that. The tone shifted in the small space between them within the car as Michelle kept looking at her.

"I realised tonight how far you've come," Michelle murmured softly. "And I wanted to acknowledge that with you tonight, if you'd be okay with it."

"Acknowledge it how?" Rory asked. She sounded wary only because this wasn't where she'd expected the conversation to go. She hadn't done anything Michelle would be proud of. It had taken her far too long to finally have the courage to speak to her mum about what had been going on for her this year, and Daphne had been the one who had made it easy tonight. Rory was glad, and grateful, but she wasn't proud of herself.

"I took BDSM off the table for the reasons I told you," Michelle said. She dipped her chin and watched Rory very carefully. "I'd like to look at putting it back on the table again. If that's something you want."

Rory tried to stay very aware of her facial expression, of her body language, knowing

Michelle was watching all of it and the slightest shift could give away her feelings. Rory wanted to be sure of her own feelings before her girlfriend read them.

"I… Are you sure?" Rory said, instead of answering immediately. The query was partially to buy herself more time, partially to triple check.

Michelle looked sure. She nodded. Her gaze was piercing. Rory held her breath.

"Okay," she whispered. "I mean, yes. I would like that. A lot."

The car remained thick with words left unspoken. Michelle said nothing more until they returned home. Rory tried not to squirm too much in her seat.

When the Michelle opened up the car door and the light came on inside, Rory saw how much she'd failed in keeping her squirming to herself. There was a sardonic smile on Michelle's lips and a twinkle in her eye that she deliberately made sure Rory saw before she stepped out of the car and came around the other side.

Rory was just stepping out of her side of the car when she saw Michelle's hand extended down to her.

"Come now," she said, and Rory was helpless to do anything other than take Michelle's hand and come with her.

Her body began to shake in anticipation as they crossed the threshold to Michelle's bedroom, Rory's hand still in hers.

They stood before each other.

"You're ready to do this," Michelle said.

"I am. More than ready," Rory said confidently. "Where do you want me?"

The corner of Michelle's lip quirked, but her answer wasn't given in words. Instead, she let go Rory's hand and walked around the other girl until she was standing behind Rory. Instinctively, Rory knew not to move, not to turn her head, or body, to follow Michelle's stride.

"You're like a gift I get to unwrap." Michelle trailed a single finger from shoulder blade to hip bone above the clothes. Although they'd both touched each other in far more intimate ways, the light touch and the promise of what it held caused Rory to shudder. "So responsive," Michelle purred.

This was where Rory usually would have quipped her way through, but it didn't feel right. The whole room seemed slow down. Rory felt keenly aware of exactly where she was standing and where Michelle was in relation to her as she came to stand by Rory's side. Was this the way that Michelle usually viewed the world, with that keen, analytical way she had?

Michelle's hand pressed against Rory's abdomen. "Breathe," she said. And then Rory's breathing became part of the keen awareness Rory had of the room.

In. Hold. Out. Hold. A perfectly even pattern. In. Hold. Out. Hold.

"Good," Michelle crooned, close to her ear. Rory could feel the wisps of her hair flutter at Michelle's breath. Her lips parted and, for a second, she lost the perfect rhythm of her breathing.

God, how was she already this turned on? Michelle had hardly even touched her yet. Certainly not in a way that was overtly sexual.

Michelle's hand lifted from her stomach just after Rory had regained her even breath. Again, she strode behind her. Rory felt like that was even more titillating. She had no idea where the next touch, next sensation, or order, was coming from. She did her best to remain completely still, to breathe as instructed, and nothing more.

Michelle's fingers slid under the tee that Rory wore. Rory closed her eyes at the sweet touch of her girlfriend's fingers against her skin, smiling as that touch turned into one that had nails scraping in a downward motion as she'd done to Rory's arm the night of the party. Her back was far more sensitive than her arm, and Rory shuddered out a gasp. When Michelle's hands started to raise a second time, it was with the tee coming up with them.

"Lift your arms," Michelle murmured, and Rory did exactly that. The cool air in the room combined with the new feeling of exposure. The scene caused bumps over her stomach and ribs to rise. The only thing she was wearing above the waist once her tee was removed was a plain, black sports bra.

Again, that was nothing Michelle hadn't seen before.

"Face me."

For the first time, Rory got to directly see Michelle's features in this moment. Her voice was deeper and more commanding than was usual, but even that hadn't prepared her for the lazy lidded gaze of her girlfriend, the minutely parted lips as she gazed at Rory as though she was a toy specifically placed for Michelle to enjoy.

"Do you enjoy being on display for me?" Michelle asked, lifting her chin, and Rory wanted to nod, wanted to agree immediately so there could be no doubting that what Michelle wanted, Rory was happy to give.

"Oh yes," she breathed.

The smile that curled Michelle's lips was different from her usual one. Her eyes still smiled with the lips, but the creases didn't change the almost predatory light that rested there.

"I want you to remove your bra," she told Rory.

"Yes, Miss," Rory murmured without thinking.

"Stop."

Rory did.

Michelle took a step closer and raised Rory's chin with the side of her forefinger and thumb. "We haven't talked about labels for while we're in scenes. Is that what you would like to call me?"

Rory just looked at Michelle.

"Miss?" Michelle prompted.

Ah. "If it pleases you," Rory answered.

"It does." Again, that little smile that hardly changed her eyes. "And what would you like to be called within these moments between us?" she asked.

Rory hadn't thought of that. She didn't have an answer prepared.

"Well," said Michelle, after waiting a few seconds. "We'll come back to that. I believe you were removing your bra."

As Rory's tee and bra lay abandoned on the floor, Rory stood topless in front of Michelle. She had never felt more beautiful. Michelle's fingers touched and stroked her as her eyes craved and worshiped every inch that they touched. As her fingers teased and tweaked Rory's nipples, Rory thought she would cry out and come from the exquisite pain and pleasure.

"No, that's not too much for you at all, is it?" Michelle murmured, testing out Rory's boundaries, and looking time and again to Rory's features to read what was written on them. She pinched her right nipple, then leaned forward to steal the gasp out of Rory's mouth with a kiss. Rory's whole body pressed into Michelle's, not even dissuaded as the pressure around the sensitive nub grew more intense.

And when it released, the absence of that pressure created a new sensation that rocked her. Rory panted, all hope of even breaths having gone out the window long since, and Michelle was cool, calm, collected... and pleased.

"On the bed," she told her girlfriend, and Rory leapt to obey.

She'd already known that Michelle was talented with her fingers and mouth, but when commands were added into the rest of it—leaving Rory sometimes panting on the bed while not allowed to move her arms, or not allowed to reach up to touch Michelle—Rory felt like everything between them rose to an even more heightened level.

Afterwards, Michelle held Rory in her arms as her body gradually returned to normal.

"This is what we call aftercare," Michelle said, her fingers stroking through Rory's hair.

"Whatever it is," Rory said drowsy with pleasure, "I like it."

"I thought you might." Michelle's fingers moved through Rory's hair for several moments, neither woman saying anything. Then, "You enjoyed it all, then?"

"Oh, yes." Rory could barely keep her eyes open, but she could keep her attention on this conversation if the alternative was that Michelle might think she hadn't been 100% okay with everything that had just happened over the last hour. "I can't believe we waited to do that for so long. That was... out of this world."

Michelle chuckled, and Rory could feel the vibration of the sound through her ear being pressed to Michelle's diaphragm.

"We waited to make sure you would enjoy it this much," Michelle reminded her softly.

Rory was nodding along with Michelle's words, but she was starting to lose focus in the conversation. A part of her felt a bit bad about it. "You put so much effort into that scene... Did you... enjoy it?"

Another rumble of laughter. "Oh yes. It was everything I wanted and more."

"What's it like for you?" Rory murmured curiously.

"Hm?"

"Well, I mean, I had all those sensations, all those *orgasms*." Rory's voice grew luxurious and warm with the recent memory of them.

"You talk as if I didn't come as well," Michelle said. She sounded amused.

"Well, I mean, but... It's different. You spent so much more time on me. I just worry there wasn't as much in it for you as there was for me."

"You mean, apart from being able to coax the expression of that much pleasure from you? From seeing you completely under my control? Surrendering? I don't think you've ever seen how gorgeous you are when you orgasm." Rory blushed, but Michelle seemed thoughtful. "Maybe we should do it in front of a mirror next time."

"Oh god!" Rory exclaimed, simultaneously shamed and warmed by the thought of it. It was something she'd never done before. But now that

Michelle had mentioned it, she couldn't stop picturing it. They might start in the shower, sudsing each other's bodies with the lavender body wash Michelle kept in there. Rinsing under the spray before Michelle commanded her to dip down to her knees and take Michelle's nipples into her mouth…

Rory couldn't *believe* it when the warm spot between her legs clenched achingly with another moment of need.

"Well," Michelle said, after some thought. "It's like what I said this morning: I like being able to give people a pleasant experience. Whether that's stroking hair, or…"

"Or plying someone with many, many orgasms?" Rory finished archly.

Michelle strokes turned into a playful pinch before going back to languorous stroking, but still Rory twitched and yelped. "Complain again, and I'll take them away," she said, mock seriously.

"I'll be good," Rory said, just as mockingly meek.

"See that you do," Michelle growled, before giving her a loving kiss on the top of her head.

Rory closed her eyes, then opened them again. She didn't care to fall asleep too quickly. She wanted to savour this night, this moment, as long as she could. At the moment, the idea of an all night stay up and talk wasn't completely out of the question.

At the same time, her eyelids were starting to

have other ideas.

"So... with aftercare... could there be bedtime stories?" Rory asked.

"That depends," Michelle said, turning her head to the side to get a glimpse of Rory's face. "Are you asking for a bedtime story right now?"

The smile on her lips was too wide for her to get away with appearing coy.

"Very well," said Michelle, indulgently. "I see no reason why not. Once upon a time..."

Chapter Nineteen

Everything was amazing. Everything was beyond fantastic. She couldn't remember the last time she'd felt that everything was as fine as this.

How're things?

It wasn't the first time Helena had texted her over the holidays, but it was the first time in about a week. Rory leapt on her phone in her excitement to reply.

Pretty crazy weekend, she replied, coming back to the bed with her phone and leaning her head on Michelle's shoulder for a moment as she replied. *Kinda fantastic in the end. How about you?*

I think I've met someone!!! Helena's reply was almost immediate and clearly excited.

Rory chuckled. Michelle looked up at her from the book she was reading, but Rory waved it away just saying, "Helena."

Her thumbs flew across the keyboard, eager to involve herself in her housemate's joy for a few minutes before bed. *Who is it?*

A guy who goes to our uni, he came up to Wilson's Prom with some friends.

The phone slipped from Rory fingers, falling onto the duvet between she and Michelle. She almost didn't have the courage to pick it up and type in the next message. *What's his name?*

His name's Matt.

"You all right?" Michelle reached out and touched her hand.

Rory put her phone down, face down, on the bedside table. Then she paused. She didn't want to lie to Michelle, but she just wasn't ready to go into it right now. Not this close to bed. "Do you mind if we talk about it later? I think I'd rather head to sleep now."

Michelle gazed at her a moment. Rory met her gaze, and saw the moment when Michelle decided against pursuing it. "Later it is," she said, her fingers moving again to stroke along the top of Rory's thigh. "Sure I can't convince you to stay up a bit longer?"

Truthfully, that was the last thing Rory wanted with the thoughts that were currently running around in her head.

"Tomorrow night?" she asked, leaning across to kiss her girlfriend.

Michelle drew her forefinger down over Rory's cheekbone and the hollow of her cheek. "I'll hold you to that."

Michelle fell asleep before she did. The lamps were lit on either side of the bed. Rory reached around to turn off the one closest to her, but she didn't want to disturb Michelle by leaning over her, and she didn't want to leave the circle of Michelle's arms to get out of bed and turn it off that way.

She kissed Michelle's arm lovingly, and had the satisfaction of an answering and contented moan in Michelle's sleep. She took a deep breath, and tried to sleep.

~~*

Rory looked at the clock. It was four a.m., or close enough. She couldn't call Jason, couldn't wake Michelle, and Helena—

She didn't know if she would ever walk into her dorm again on pain of running into her housemate or having to hear about Matt.

Over the course of the early hours of morning, she'd decided to drop out or defer uni three separate times.

That was ridiculous, of course, her saner mind told her. But what was she supposed to do? She was, only just, a recovering alcoholic, former abuse victim, and her housemate…

Rory also got up to vomit three separate times over the course of the early morning. By the end, it was just dry retching.

Around six a.m., Rory heard Michelle's alarm go off in her bedroom. Several minutes later, her girlfriend came out of the bedroom looking for her and looking confused.

"There you are," she said, kissing her good morning. "Why are you up so early?"

There was no honest way for Rory to answer that. Not if she wanted Michelle to go to work.

"Couldn't sleep," she murmured, curling close to Michelle.

"Is this to do with what you weren't ready to talk about last night?" Michelle tipped her head to the side.

The concern in her eyes threatened to undo Rory. Instead of trying to speak, she just nodded her head.

"Sweetheart..." Michelle started.

"Not before work," Rory said. They didn't have time to go into this now. And Rory didn't know if she could hold herself together while Michelle was at work if they opened this can or worms now. She met her girlfriend's gaze with sincerity. "As soon as you get home tonight, though. We'll talk about it then, all right?"

Michelle glanced her up and down slowly before nodding her head. "As soon as I get home," she agreed. "But try to get some sleep during the day. And call Jason after you wake up."

It was good advice. "I will," Rory promised.

After Michelle left for work, Rory lay on Michelle's side of the bed—which she imagined was still warm from her girlfriend's body—and tried to clear her thoughts.

After a couple of hours of that, Rory thought to call Jason from the bedroom. But before she did that, another thought came to her. She'd talked to Jason before, albeit briefly, about her abuse. She'd come out of that feeling like it would be a good idea to talk to someone else who was a professional in that field, rather than someone who had experience in alcohol abuse.

Flicking across to the internet app on her phone, she started searching for counsellors, psychologists, anyone with a speciality in sexual abuse or assault.

She found a couple of practicing psychologists who specialised in both sexual and substance abuse. Then she spent the next hour trying to work up the courage to call one of them. Thankfully, by that time, it was within clinic opening hours.

The first one had a hold line that broke her nerves before she came through to an actual receptionist. She hung up. Sighed. Looked at her phone for the next on the list.

It rang. Three times in total. Rory was as aware of them as she was of her heartbeats.

"Good morning, Somerset Medical Clinic, this is Rosemary speaking."

Rory's mouth went dry.

"Hello?"

"Hello." Rory's voice sounded husky, cracked, and she said the word again in case Rosemary hadn't heard her the first time.

"Good morning. How can I help you?"

The voice on the other end of the phone was unerringly professional. Rory tried to pull herself together.

"I… was wanting to make an appointment with the psychologist."

"All right. What day would you like to come in?"

"Any... any day," Rory temporised.

There was the sound of clicking, like keys on a keyboard, and then Rosemary said, "We've had a late cancellation for this afternoon. Will 3:30 be a good time for you?"

"Yes." Rory didn't allow herself to worry that she answered too quickly. She'd already looked up the location and the bus route from Michelle's house to the clinic. That she could get in on the same day that she called was better than she'd dared to hope.

"Have you been here before, sweetheart?" It was the first dip in professionalism from Rosemary's voice thus far, and Rory felt herself smile and start to relax in response to it.

"No," she answered.

"Okay, I just need to get some details over the phone. And if you could arrive maybe ten minutes early today, we just have a form we'll need you to fill out."

Rosemary went through the questions she needed to ask, and then detailed the items of ID and such that Rory would need to bring with her to the appointment. Rory thanked Rosemary for her kindness, then texted Michelle to let her know about the appointment.

She got a phone call from her girlfriend during her lunch break.

"I'm proud of you," Michelle said softly, as

soon as Rory answered.

"Thank you," Rory said.

"Tell me all about it when I get home?"

"I already promised, didn't I?"

"I'm just making sure."

They spoke a bit about Michelle's day, the time that she expected to get home, and what they wanted to do for dinner that night. Around that time, Michelle needed to sign off if she wanted to eat her lunch before getting to the end of her break.

"I—" Michelle cut herself off abruptly. Then, "I'll see you tonight."

"You will," Rory said.

She made lunch for herself, wrote up a shopping list to get on the way back from her appointment, read a little more of the book she'd borrowed from Michelle.

Then she called Jason.

Jason didn't answer his phone straight away. He couldn't sometimes, due to his work. But he'd said that his manager was pretty good with him taking phone calls from her; she understood he was a sponsor, and he didn't let it interfere too much with his work.

About a minute after she'd called him, Jason called her back. "Sorry," he said. "Was with a customer. And they didn't even buy anything! Bleh. Anyway. How are you?"

Rory liked how he did this. Never made a big deal of when she called him over what was likely a big deal.

"I, um, made an appointment with a psychologist this afternoon," she said.

"Well, good for you!" Jason replied. "When's that for?"

"This afternoon."

She could almost see his eyes bug slightly from his face. "This afternoon? I know people who have waited *weeks* to see a psych. Wow. Hope it's a good fit for you. Well, even if it's not, you haven't wasted much time in finding out."

"The receptionist seemed nice," Rory said.

"That's a good sign," Jason answered.

"And it's not too hard to get to from Michelle's place."

"That'll help keep down your stress on the way."

"That and the book I'm reading."

"Ooooh. Is this the book you were telling me that had the BDSM characters in it? You sure that's safe to read on a bus?"

Rory laughed. "I'll try to keep myself under control."

"It'll keep you distracted anyway!"

The two of them laughed comfortably. Rory tried to use the time to segue into what she wanted to say. It didn't help that she didn't know exactly what she wanted to say. She was kind of making it up as she went along, knowing that she was meant to call her sponsor when she came across problems, but not knowing how he was supposed to help with this one.

After the laughter came the silence.

"There's no alcohol in the house," Rory said baldly.

"Of course," Jason answered easily. "Michelle wouldn't do that to you."

Rory nodded silently. That was true.

She sighed. "I'm trying to keep myself distracted. Calling the psych. Reading a book. Making a shopping list. Calling you. If I do all those things, I'm not thinking about drinking."

"Distraction can be very helpful," Jason said, sounding about as mocking as he always did when he sounded like he was quoting from an AA handbook. "As can a sense of purpose."

"Well, I have that," Rory said. "In uni. Except it's school holidays now."

Jason waited for her to go on.

She heaved another sigh. "And also uni is just seeming like it's more and more problematic. Everyone drinks. Or parties. Or hangs out with someone who parties. And now, on top of that, Helena might be interested in Matt."

Just the sound of his name slithering from between her lips made her want to gag.

"Helena's your housemate, right?" Jason clarified. He didn't ask who Matt was. Both Michelle and Jason had probably memorised the name so they would never have to ask her to clarify on that point.

"Yeah," replied Rory.

"I can see how that would be difficult."

"There's no alcohol in that house either." Rory was aiming to sound chipper, but knew she sounded flat. "What if he comes over, Jason? How am I going to face that?"

"Have you tried talking to Helena about it?"

"What if she doesn't believe me?" Rory burst out. "She already puts up with so much from me! I can't... I just can't imagine having that conversation. Especially not through text! And who knows what it'll be like by the end of holidays."

"She might not be interested in him anymore." Jason said it quietly. But there was also something behind his words that he wasn't saying. Rory heard it too.

"You don't think he would...?"

She couldn't finish the question. She didn't need Jason to answer it either. Both of them sat in charged silence for a moment longer.

"I have to say something, don't I?" Her voice sounded very, very small.

"If she's your friend, she'll hear that you're concerned about her," Jason offered, just as quietly.

Rory felt a shudder run through her entire body. "I don't... I don't know how..."

"Why don't you see if you could call her?" Jason asked. "A lot of things get lost in text."

It was a good idea. Rory just had to psyche herself up for it.

She kind of wanted to get it out of the way before she went to her psychologist appointment in the afternoon. At least then, if it all blew up in her face with Helena, she'd have someone to talk it over with before she exploded all over Michelle.

Are you available for a phone call?

Rory looked at the text message she had ready for Helena, stared at it for several moments with her thumb hovering over the SEND button. Well, it was going to do no good to her in her drafts folder. Rory closed her eyes and pressed her thumb down. Okay. It was done now. No way she could take it back. She opened her eyes again. The words she'd written were sitting there in front of her, a grey speech bubble around them.

Rory got up and made herself a cup of coffee.

When she came back, there was already a reply on her screen: *Yeah, okay.*

With trembling fingers, Rory selected the dial option.

"Hey Rory, how's your holidays?"

Helena's familiar voice fell into her ear, and Rory just wanted to forget the reasons she'd decided to call. It would be so, so easy just to say she'd missed hearing from her housemate over the several week break so far.

"It's been really great. Been spending a lot of it at Michelle's."

"Aww, fantastic. I'm so glad that you guys managed to make up," Helena said.

"Yeah." Rory's throat tightened up as she made

the attempt to at least turn the conversation in the direction she'd meant it to go, "So how has your holiday been so far?"

"Oh, good. Mum's been a bit of a pain. I didn't visit enough during semester, apparently."

"And... Matt?" Rory asked hesitantly. "The guy you messaged me about?"

"Oh, yeah, he's good," Helena said evasively.

Rory wasn't really sure how to work with that. Was it better that she didn't sound excited about talking about him? Did that mean she wasn't interested in him anymore? Or had something darker happened?

"Really? I mean... you can tell me... if you want," Rory said, not sure how much she wanted to hear, but unable to keep herself from at least making the offer.

Helena sighed into the handset, and Rory heard it like a whoosh of wind in her ear. "Well, he said some pretty crummy things about you," Helena said eventually.

"About... *me*?" Rory demanded. What on earth bad things did he have to say about her? The last time she saw him, he'd apologised to her for being a dick!

Helena hesitated some more. "He found out that you were my housemate, and he already knew you had a substance abuse problem..."

"He... he said that?" Rory asked, finding this more and more unbelievable as it went on.

"Mm. I mean, I think that rumours have made

it out to be worse than it is. You're not on drugs as well, are you?"

"Helena!" This conversation was *not* going the way Rory had thought it would. Her heart was pounding hard. "You know me better than that!"

"Well, I didn't know you had a drinking problem until Tally said…" Helena explained defensively. "I mean, it was kinda possible."

Rory bit back another argument. If Helena was already sounding defensive, there was no point. Rory hung her head and just said nothing.

"Rory?" Helena said, a moment later. "Are you still there?"

"Still here," Rory mumbled.

"I told him that what he said about drugs wasn't true anyway," Helena said, as though that made it better, more like she was on Rory's side, rather than the side of her abuser.

"Thanks," Rory said, not really feeling it.

"Are you mad?"

"Do I sound mad?"

"Well… it's hard to tell over the phone. But, yeah, you do a little bit."

Rory gritted her teeth. "I just expected to be talking to my housemate about our holidays, not about my possible drug habit."

This time Helena went silent.

Rory didn't want to back down; *couldn't* back down, cause that would be like saying that Matt was right. And he wasn't right. About any of it.

"Look, Matt had sex with me one night when I

wasn't sober enough to make the decision. If he's saying shitty things about me, maybe it's because he knows he did something wrong. Maybe don't pay too much attention to it." It wasn't coming out like Rory had wanted. She heard the words coming out of her mouth, and they were spiteful, not the words of a friend who was concerned for her housemate. She didn't even want to hear Helena's reply. "Look, I've gotta go to a psych appointment to try to get help for what Matt did to me. So I'm gonna go."

She hung up, and then immediately regretted it. She should have held onto the phone call just a minute longer. Just long enough for Helena to reply. Then she would have known what Helena thought about her words, whether she believed them, whether they would be okay when semester started up again in two weeks' time.

Rory hopelessly watched her mobile, waiting for a text message from Helena that never came. After she looked at the time and realised that it was ten minutes after she'd wanted to leave for her appointment, she grabbed the phone with more violence than it deserved, shoved it into her bag and banged out of Michelle's front door.

Chapter Twenty

The receptionist was too busy to have a long chat or to allay any concerns with Rory as she arrived, so Rory just took a seat in the waiting room with the rest of the patients.

There was a boy coughing into his hand, while his mum rubbed him sympathetically on the back. The looks on everyone's faces looked as though they would rather be somewhere else. Rory very much believed the same look was currently on her features. The waiting room walls were white with smudge marks from children's fingers and the floors were stained an off-white from age that cleaning and sanitising didn't quite get out. The television was on in the corner of the room. It was playing some late daytime television soap that Rory was only interested in because it was so long since she'd watched any.

She'd been sitting for about fifteen minutes when an older man wearing an open, white coat walked into the waiting room and called her name. Rory stood up, gratefully turning away from the television and the rest of the waiting room.

"Come with me." His voice was the gentle, grandfatherly tone that some men had. He led her out of the waiting room and down a short hall before opening a door and gesturing for her to walk in before him.

There wasn't a clear seat for her and for him, no desk in front of which the psychologist would obviously sit. Rory was still looking around, trying to decide which of the three chairs she should take when the psychologist—Dr Brian Reynold, Rory remembered from his online profile—closed the door and stood in front of one of the chairs.

Well, that at least narrowed it down to two. Rory picked one hastily.

Pointedly, Dr Brian didn't down sit until she'd done so. An artefact of his generation, Rory figured.

He laid one ankle over the other knee and leaned back comfortably. "So, why don't you tell me what's brought you to see me today, Rory?"

He didn't look at his file or check her name or anything. Rory looked around the office, which had photos of people young enough to be either children or grandchildren, as well as a couple of generic wall hangings. She almost thought she could be comfortable in this environment.

"I found your profile on the internet," Rory started. "It said that you cater to substance abuse as well as... s—s..."

"Sexual abuse, yes," Dr Brian finished for her. He steepled his fingers, elbows resting on his thighs. "Is that what's brought you here today?

Issues of sexual abuse?"

Rory looked at her hands. They were shaking. She hardly trusted her voice to pull out another long sentence, so settled for just, "Yes."

"I see." Dr Brian inclined his head. He waited, or Rory assumed he waited because she still didn't look up. After a moment, he asked gently, "Do you feel able to talk to me about it?"

Rory gave a bit of a desperate chuckle. "Well, I've come here to do that, so it'd be a bit sad if I couldn't."

"This is a very difficult subject to tackle. All people react to an incident of this nature differently. It wouldn't be sad if you couldn't bring yourself to speak about it the first time. I'm still a stranger to you. Perhaps you need some time to become comfortable around me."

"That's true," Rory mumbled. After a moment, she even managed to look up at him.

"Now, that's better." He smiled, and he had a nice smile, long dimples in both cheeks and a twinkle in both eyes. "Why don't you just tell me about yourself. Are you studying? Working? Do you have a boyfriend?"

"Studying," Rory answered. These questions were easy to answer. "Not working. Mum's helping me out. I have a girlfriend, not boyfriend."

"Ah. That's very good you've got a supportive parent. Are you and your mum close?"

Rory met Dr Brian's eyes. "Very. I just told her. About my drinking. Mum was…" Rory shook her head in wonder at her remembered fears of disappointing her. "She'd offered me a glass of chardonnay. When I told her, the chardonnay went back in the fridge and was replaced by orange juice without another word."

"I'm sure it was hard for you, working up to that, not knowing how she was going to respond."

"It was."

"And it was a relief when she responded the way she did?"

"She was only the second person I chose to tell. A friend from uni. My girlfriend. Mum. They all reacted like it was okay. Like I was going to be okay. They understood. They didn't judge me."

"People often judge themselves more harshly than other people judge them," Dr Brian offered sagely. They sat together in a comfortable moment of silence, while Rory sorted through her thoughts. Then Dr Brian asked, "What about your girlfriend? Why don't you tell me about her?"

"What do you want to know?" Rory asked quietly. She didn't really want to talk about Michelle, didn't want to have it come to her mind all the reasons why she sometimes felt like she wasn't worth all the affection Michelle gave to her.

"Anything." Dr Brian splayed out his hands between them. "Whatever you'd like to tell me."

"Well, she works full time. I've been kinda living at her place since holidays broke out for uni. Been doing a lot of the grocery shopping so she won't get sick of me."

"How likely do you think it is that she'll get sick of you, Rory?"

"Not very," Rory said, getting frustrated and giving him the answer he wanted, the answer she hoped was correct. This situation seemed more complicated the more information she put into it, not less.

"Not very." Dr Brian repeated the words.

From him, the words sounded more likely. Rory wasn't quite sure how he did that. But he was right. Or she was. There was nothing in Michelle's attitude or actions that said she was growing sick of Rory. Just the opposite, actually.

Rory sighed. Far from being relieved, the realisation left her feeling frustrated. "I feel like there's always something wrong with me. Something that needs to be fixed. Something that Michelle needs to be worried about. And there's only a certain amount of time until she gets sick of that drama, even if she doesn't get sick of me specifically."

"I'm noticing a couple of recurring themes," Dr Brian said with a small smile. "Mostly there's an issue of your self-esteem, and I want to address that first: What has happened to you, the rape is not your fault. I want you to hear that."

Dr Brian held her gaze until it felt impossible to look away. He left them in a silence for a few moments, allowing his words to sink into the space between them.

"It's not my fault," Rory said softly into the

silence.

"Good. We're going to keep working on that. And perhaps you have a substance abuse problem. You're here today asking for help. Have you been going to meetings?"

"I have, yeah. I have a sponsor," Rory said.

"Good. Both of those things are very good. How are you finding that so far?"

"My sponsor? Jason? He's fantastic. He answers my calls, well, most of the time, even if he's at work. He and Michelle met each other, and they get along. I just... He doesn't... the incident with the... rape..." It was getting a little bit better each time she said it, Rory noticed. She only flinched after she said the word that time. No tightness of throat, or a feeling of sickness at the thought of the word.

"You felt you needed to find someone else to speak to about that part of your abuse," Dr Brian finished for her.

"Yes," Rory agreed. So they were back at this again. She really did have to talk about it with him. She'd kick herself afterwards if she didn't. "And I found out that my girlfriend... that she'd also been raped several years ago."

"How did that make you feel?"

"Defenceless," Rory answered. "It was like... it was bad enough that it happened to me. Did it have to happen to her as well? She's always the strong one. And seeing her falling apart while she told me about it... I couldn't... I *hate* that that happened to her."

"Of course," Dr Brian said, allaying her fears that she might have been too vehement in her description in an instant. "That's completely natural for you to feel."

Rory nodded, feeling encouraged to go on. "I look at her now, and I wonder how long it's going to take me to become strong like that. Right now, I feel so broken in so many places. If I didn't have to deal with the alcoholism as well, I think it would be one thing. But it's so much to deal with. Even with Michelle, and Jason, I'm still just one person."

"They're both two very big issues. It's normal that you feel overwhelmed," said Dr Brian.

"So I guess the magic question is how do I handle it from here?" Rory's lips twisted in a grimace. She hefted a heavy sigh at what she saw was completely unachievable.

"Another thing I'm seeing from you is your tendency towards emotional behaviours with regards to the people around you. Your feelings of angst and anger coming out about your own sexual abuse seem like they're related to the feelings you have about the same thing having happened to your girlfriend. What's your usual living situation like? When you're not on holidays. Do you have any housemates?"

Rory barked out a laugh. "My housemate," she said, full of such bitter mirth. "She texted me from Gippsland to tell me that my rapist is her latest crush."

Even saying it out loud, she somehow couldn't believe that this was her life. It just didn't seem like this many things could pack onto one person.

For the first time, Dr Brian's eyebrows lifted in some sign of emotion. "Have you told her?"

"I couldn't! He beat me to it, saying that I was addicted to drugs as well as alcohol. I'm not," Rory said quickly, anticipating the same line of questioning she'd had to battle from Helena earlier that day. Her gaze was fierce now as she met her psychologist's eyes.

"That's fine," he answered, neutral. "I'm very sorry to hear that. That must be difficult."

"Difficult is an understatement!" Rory was raising her voice now, but she couldn't help it, couldn't bring it down. This was helping. This wasn't helping. This was helping. This wasn't helping. The room seemed to be caving in around her. She tried to push her gaze out towards the window in Dr Bruce's office, but she couldn't remember where it was. She couldn't escape her thoughts, her mind. Her heart was racing too fast.

"Rory. I want you to look at me." For the first time, he shifted in his seat, bringing both feet to the floor and leaning forward "I want you to take a few deep breaths. Right now, with me."

Rory could see him in front of her, but she couldn't see how this was going to help. As he initiated the deep in and out breaths he wanted her to take, Rory began to follow him. She felt completely ridiculous as she did as he said, breathing in and out with his counting until he lay his hands back down on his legs.

"Good. I want you to reflect on how you're feeling right now," Dr Brian told her, after a couple of seconds had passed.

Her heart wasn't racing quite so hard, though Rory felt shaky from the rush of adrenaline that had flooded her. The room was back to its normal dimensions. She felt tired, and drained. But her feelings no longer overwhelmed her. She could make the choice on not *only* focusing on those emotions.

She said all of this to Dr Brian.

"I want you to take that with you," he told her. "After you leave this room. Mindfulness is just one of the techniques I think would be advantageous for you to learn to use. Our emotions are not in control of us, regardless of how it feels that way sometimes. But I want to state again that you have good reason for the ways you are feeling."

He took a piece of paper from a stack on his bookshelf, and a pen from his shirt pocket, and started to write something.

"I want to see you again in no more than one week's time. You might feel a need to come in again early, and that's okay as well. Use the support you've got with Michelle and Jason. But in the time in between now and our next session, I want you to consider writing down things you'd like to talk about in our next session. Then, even if you're feeling uncomfortable actually talking to me about it at the start, you can choose to give me the piece of paper to open the conversation for you. How do you feel about that?"

Rory nodded her head slowly. The hour had just flown and she felt... drained.

Dr Brian stood up so that he wasn't still sitting when she stood. Rory shook her head, but didn't comment.

"Thank you. For seeing me today. On short notice." She wasn't sure what to do at this point. Did she just walk out? Offer to shake his hand? Say she was looking forward to seeing him next time?

None of these things really applied. Even thanking him for having a free lot in his work schedule probably hadn't strictly speaking been necessary.

"You're welcome," he said, nonetheless.

"Um, okay. See you." Rory shrugged and slipped out of his office, back down the hall towards the waiting room. She gave the slip of paper to Rosemary, who looked a little less harried and a little more interested to see her.

"I hope your appointment went well," she said, as she started keying in the time and date of Rory's next appointment.

"It did. I think." Rory's lips twisted. Typical that the first question outside of therapy would be as difficult as some of the ones inside it.

Rosemary chucked. "It's a bit like that your first time. But he's good, though. He's very busy."

"I'm grateful that you fit me in this morning," Rory said sincerely.

"Always happy to do what I can," Rosemary answered. She held out the time and date of the next available appointment with Dr Brian. Rory took it, glanced at the details and put the card into her pocket.

"Thanks. See you then," she said, before shuffling out of the clinic.

The setting sun zeroed in on her, a bright disk glaring over the top of the building at the end of the street as Rory walked towards the bus stop. It wasn't that it was hot, it was that it was violently present. She shaded her eyes with her hand as best she could but, by the time she was sitting at the shelter, her eyes felt incredibly strained. She was glad that it wasn't a long walk from the bus stop at the other end to Michelle's house. Between the glaring sun and the aftereffects of her first therapy session, Rory began to feel exhausted. She only had one thing more to do on the way home, but thankfully the grocery list wasn't overly long.

She got home about ten minutes before the front door opened again. The noise from the street included sunset singing birds and Michelle's calling through the house, "Hello?"

"Hey, darling." She'd had time to put the groceries away and so didn't have to worry about leaving perishables out on the bench while she walked up the hall to greet her girlfriend with a hug. "How was your day at work?"

"Woeful," Michelle said, kissing Rory as she put down her purse, then pulled Rory closer to kiss her more deeply. "I was thinking of you all day."

"Hey! I'd like to think that'd make things better, not worse." Rory had to work on her affronted tone of voice. It was about as woeful as Michelle's day had been. Obviously both of them knew what Michelle was referencing.

Michelle tipped her head to the side. "Usually. Yes. Of course. But you know—"

"Please," Rory said, dropping all pretence in a second. "I'm not ready to talk about that just yet."

Michelle lifted her chin. "Say no more." She stole another kiss, then pressed Rory to the wall. She kept enough distance between them that she could see Rory's face clearly, but Rory was in bliss from the second Michelle's authoritative hold grasped her upper arms and moved her. Michelle kissed her girlfriend's mouth greedily, coaxing her mouth open and darting her tongue in between the lips. Rory gasped into Michelle's mouth as Michelle's hands found the soft skin above her jeans but under her tops. Her fingers completely distracted her when they tucked under the waist line, then crept along to the top button of the jeans, kissing her all the time.

The top button was undone. Rory moaned, leaned towards Michelle and—

Michelle stepped away. Suddenly, all that was holding Rory up was the wall behind her. She opened her eyes, feeling wonderfully hazy, but confused to see Michelle standing about a foot away from her, droopy eyed and a salacious look on her lips.

"Tease," Rory croaked.

"I am what I am," Michelle said, with no small amount of satisfaction. She then took Rory's hand and led them both into the kitchen.

Chapter Twenty-one

She waited until after dinner that night, knowing her appetite would vanish as soon as she started to talk. Out of conscientiousness, she also waited till Michelle had finished. She was sitting on the bar stool as Michelle finished off the dishes.

"Helena's interested in Matt." The words fell into the space in between them, ruining the comfortable mood between them.

Michelle picked up the tea towel from the oven rail and dried her hands.

"I don't know if they're dating. Or whatever. I spoke to her on the phone today. He's already said some shitty things about me." Rory rolled her eyes. She was starting to get to the point where she was running out of tears. "I honestly don't know what I'd do if I was at home rather than here."

She was just so sick of fighting. At that moment, she felt apathetic enough that she was worried about what she'd do if she weren't here in Michelle's house. It was a fairly awful way to feel. Not necessarily craving the alcohol, but not particularly inclined to fight the addiction either.

Just as she'd anticipated, the food she'd eaten was spoiling in her stomach. She wouldn't be eating dessert tonight.

"So that's what was happening this morning. Well, the phone call happened during the day today. But I got the text message that he was in Gippsland—and that she was interested in him—last night."

Michelle came around the counter and put her arms around Rory. "Sweetheart, you should have woken me up."

"You had work this morning," Rory said.

Michelle tightened her arms just a little around her. "You should have woken me up."

"Fine," Rory said. "Next time my housemate tells me she's interested in… I'll wake you up."

"Good." Michelle's front pressed against Rory's back and Rory relaxed against her body, finding comfort in her girlfriend wrapped around her. "Is it very hard for you to get to uni from here?" she asked, stroking her hand up and down Rory's arm.

Rory shook her head, hair brushing against Michelle's collarbone. "No. Not at all."

Michelle kissed the back of her head. "Because it would be fine with me if you wanted to keep on staying here."

Rory turned around to look at the expression on Michelle's face as she leaned forward. "What…?" Was Michelle saying what she thought she was saying?

"Shit…" Michelle leaned her forehead against Rory's, giving a self-deprecating shake of the head. "I told myself I wouldn't do this again."

"Do what?" Rory's lips curved even though she wasn't truly aware of what Michelle was talking about, but wanting to be part of the joke, whatever it was.

Michelle's eyelashes butterflied up and Rory looked into her girlfriend's gaze.

"Wouldn't... fall in love again."

As Michelle's breath touched her face, Rory felt the bottom fall from her heart. That was hardly a joke. She stared longer into Michelle's eyes. There certainly wasn't any laughter there now, nothing self-deprecating. Her heart was in her eyes as well as on her sleeve, and Rory believed her.

For the next few moments, the only sounds in the room were their inward and outward breathing.

Rory felt selfish to have been too absorbed in her own problems that she hadn't noticed the signs before now.

"I'd hoped..." Rory started, happy tears now springing to her eyes.

Michelle reached out and took the tear onto her forefinger before it fell too far. "Should I take this to mean you love me too?" she asked in a soft, very indulgent voice.

Rory nodded her head eagerly, butting her forehead against Michelle before sitting back enough to give them both space. "Yes, I do," she said. "I really do."

Michelle didn't allow her to keep her space long after that. Bringing her close, she kissed her long and longingly. They were both laughing and grabbing for each other, and didn't make it as far as the bedroom before clothes came off.

~~*

"Benefits of living in a house by yourself," Michelle said.

Rory lay on Michelle's chest, listening to the sound of her girlfriend's heartbeat under her ear. It was gradually slowing down.

"Not any more, if I take up your offer," Rory murmured testingly.

Michelle's arms tightened around her, and her voice sounded husky as she said, "Not in that case, no. I don't really see you minding if I walk around the house naked, though."

"True."

They were both silent for a moment, content in each other's company and the lethargy that came after sex.

"I'm a terrible girlfriend. I completely derailed your day with my proclamation of love," Michelle said after a moment.

"Believe me, your proclamation was very welcome," Rory said. The troubles of Helena and Matt seemed so far away now, and that was exactly where Rory wanted them to stay. When she didn't move to restart any of those topics,

Michelle allowed that subject to drop in favour of another.

"Just... Don't hurt me, okay?" she said, showing Rory one of those rare moments of vulnerability.

Rory lifted her head from Michelle's chest. "Where did that come from?" she asked.

Not moving from her place on the pillow, Michelle shrugged. "Nothing you've done," she assured her. "I just want to make sure you... keep talking to me. About what's important to you. Even if things change. I'd rather know."

The more Rory got to know Michelle, the more she guessed that there was more to the ex-girlfriend before her, and to the guy who had raped Michelle. But that was Michelle's story, and Rory had too many scars of her own to think she could blunder into Michelle's past and make anything better.

"Of course," she said instead, reaching out to cup her girlfriend's jaw, thumbing her lower lip. "I wouldn't do things any other way. I'll keep talking to you. I promise to do my best never to hurt you."

~~*

It was a week before semester two classes were due to start, and Rory came back to her house grabbing another backpack of her things she'd rather not be left in a place where Matt might invade. She still hadn't decided yet whether or not she was planning to move in officially with Michelle or just stay with her until she found somewhere else she could afford on her student income. It hadn't come up again so far. Rory didn't want to make a final decision either way until she'd at least spoken to Helena in person.

But she wasn't intending was to do that a week before classes were set to start. She thought Helena was still in Gippsland.

When the front door opened, and Rory had her back to it, she spun around with her whole body tensing. As Helena walked in, Rory braced herself to see Matt behind her.

She couldn't quite help the sigh of relief that escaped her lips when he wasn't there.

Helena met her eyes, then looked away.

"I didn't know you'd be here," she said in a low voice, immediately turning back to the door and focusing an inordinate amount of attention in closing it.

"It's my house too," Rory said defensively.

"I know." Helena was defensive as well. "But it's a week before classes."

"Yes," Rory agreed. "It is."

For a long while, there was silence between the two girls. They hadn't been so stilted since Rory started dating Michelle. Thinking back on them, Rory wasn't sure they'd even been this stilted with each other then. Her hand was still holding tight to the strap of her backpack, but she didn't feel the need to run now that Matt hadn't walked in. Her phone was in her pocket. Both Jason and Michelle were a text message away. But she didn't reach for it, not yet.

Helena had stopped looking at the door and was staring back at Rory. Almost as though she felt she had to say something now that she'd been caught staring, Helena said, "I don't know how to talk to you."

"Well, I'm still me," Rory said.

"Yeah. You're that girl who kinda dropped off the face of the earth when she got a girlfriend, and who ended up being an alcoholic."

Rory tightened her jaw. She looked away first, and then left the room to grab her things from the bathroom.

Unexpectedly, Helena followed her there. "I mean, tell me what you'd do if you were me," she said, standing against the doorframe. "There's this guy I like. Who I haven't met before, but we go to the same uni. It seems perfect. His friends are nice. Then he finds out that you're my housemate and, yeah, he says some things. Some of them I already know are true."

Rory felt trapped in the small room, unable to get out without bumping into Helena or pushing her out the way.

"Wouldn't you even be a little bit curious to know if he was right about the other things? Are you really going to judge me for that?" Helena had her arms crossed against her chest. This sounded like a conversation she'd already rehearsed her part of on the way back from Gippsland.

No, that wasn't fair. But neither was the fact that Rory hadn't rehearsed anything for this.

"Please get out of my way," she said in a low voice, ducking her head.

"Please answer me," Helena said. There was something soft and vulnerable in her expression, in the way she said 'please', but Rory wasn't able to hear it.

"What do you want me to say? Matt didn't rape me? I imagined it all? It's completely fine if you want to date him? If he comes here? Cause, yeah, it's my place too. What if I didn't have anywhere else to go? I'm sorry we didn't talk that much after I first started dating Michelle, but that wasn't only my fault either."

She did push past Helena in the end, desperate to get out of the bathroom with her back pressed against the sink. Helena looked too shocked to react.

Rory gritted her teeth and grabbed her bag. The rest of the stuff wasn't important. Maybe she could get someone else to pick it up.

She walked straight past Helena on her way out through the living room, slamming the front door behind her. The door didn't open again; Helena never called out down the driveway after her.

Rory was glad of it.

She walked a long way out of her way to get to

the bus stop to try to cool down, probably further than she needed to walk, but the exercise was good for her. It gave her something to do with the nervous energy suffusing her entire body. She pushed herself to walk fast, faster, until she was power walking and people were giving her strange looks. She didn't care.

Chapter Twenty-two

Michelle suggested coming with Rory back to the house to get the last of her stuff that weekend.

"You like Helena," she reminded her. "Even if she's got terrible taste in guys, you still like her."

Rory had to admit grudgingly that Michelle was right. But she didn't dislike her girlfriend's protectiveness over her one bit.

Rory sent Helena a text message saying she was heading over, what time and day, and got an affirmative response two days before they got into Michelle's car to head over.

When they arrived, Helena was in her room. She came out to meet them in the living room almost as soon as Rory pushed open the front door. Michelle stayed by the front door, at Rory's back.

"Hey…" Helena started, with only a quick glance towards Michelle.

"Hey." Rory looked down, looked over at the couch, looked anywhere except at Helena for about ten seconds. Then she met her gaze, realising it was stupid to try to hide from her while they were both standing in the living room. Michelle had been right. She did like Helena. But, looking at her now, Rory wondered if this was like

Smithy all over again.

Was she just doomed to end all of her friendships from the period of her life that she was so determined to move past?

"I really don't feel great about our last conversation," Helena said in a small voice.

"I don't either," Rory admitted quietly. She hadn't come here bearing the decision to stop talking to Helena after this. But she also couldn't think of a single thing to say.

Helena pressed her lips together, then looked over at Michelle. It was obvious that just having her standing in the doorway was making her nervous. Helena shifted on her feet, sighed, and then said, "Look, I know you wouldn't just make up something like that about someone else," she said in a rush.

Rory closed her eyes and found her mouth forming the words, "Thank you." She hadn't realised how much she needed to hear the validation from her housemate, the person she'd lived with for the past year, until she heard it.

Helena smiled, but it was a sad smile. "Of course. So I get that something non-consensual went down between you and Matt."

Rory eyed Helena. She had the feeling of a 'but' sitting heavily in the air.

"But," Helena said eventually, her gaze flickering briefly to Michelle again. "There are two sides to every story. I wasn't there that night. I can't possibly know what happened between you.

And, I'll be honest: the alcohol really complicates things. But I get that you don't feel safe around him so... Since it's not okay with you, I won't invite him back to our house. Cause you were right. It is both of ours."

Rory exhaled. Reminded herself to inhale again. Again, she was very aware of Michelle standing behind her, not saying anything. Was she aware of how tense Rory was? Probably. That was exactly why Michelle had offered to come here with her today.

The more important question really was: Was Helena aware that what she offered didn't actually fix everything? That, even now, Rory was waiting for another equivocating 'but' that would completely undo even that small gesture? Her shoulders felt like they were up around her ears. Rory hardly felt as though she had taken a full, deep breath since she'd walked into the house.

"I get where you're coming from," Rory said, when she could speak. She closed her eyes, willing the words to come to her mouth while she wasn't staring at Helena. Hoping that those words wouldn't somehow make her sound like she was the bad guy, the unreasonable guy, here. "But it's not enough. I can't... I can't even deal with the idea of Matt being around *you*."

Rory opened her eyes in time to see Helena opening her mouth to speak, but surprised herself by cutting her housemate off.

"When I called you, when you were still in

Gippsland? I was calling you to make sure you were all right. I was worried Matt was going to hurt you." Rory saw the irate expression on Helena's face turn into something else. She couldn't allow herself to stop and try to process that. "I wanted to check up on you. To warn you not to drink around him. And then…" Rory shook her head. It all of a sudden became too much.

And then Helena had accused Rory of being on drugs as well. Had pointed out how some of what Matt had said was true, so the rest of it must be as well.

The words hung heavily between them. They both recollected the recent phone conversation.

If Helena hadn't known what to say before, it was nothing when compared to now. She opened and closed her mouth, emotions crossing over her face rapidly, a slight shake to her head as though she would explain something to them, but nothing came out.

Rory gazed at the floor. When Helena still said nothing, Rory realised there was nothing for it than to take the conversation to its logical conclusion. "I'm still worried about you. But I can't… be here. Around you. Around him. Even if he's not in the house with us, it's still too close."

She felt Michelle start to step towards her in support. Rory looked over her shoulder at Michelle and shook her head. She needed to take care of this on her own. She needed to know she'd at least done her very best to get her point across to Helena before she walked away.

"I wish I could be happy for you... with Matt," Rory finished, looking Helena in the eye. All she saw was that lonely girl who had been so scared that nobody wanted to be around her. Just like Rory had felt. She would have been over the moon for her if it had been anyone else. "I just can't."

"I... understand," Helena said. There was a furrow between her eyebrows were there hadn't been before, and she chewed on her lower lip like she did whenever she was thinking.

Rory waited, to see if there was anything else Helena would say afterwards. Finally, she shrugged. She had done the best she could.

"I'll see you around on campus, I guess," Rory said, more to fill in the silence than anything else.

"Yeah, of course, you will," Helena echoed.

Instead of saying anything more, Rory broke the stalemate by turning around to spend the next few minutes grabbing stuff she'd missed on previous visits and putting them in her bag while Helena either watched on or turned away. Rory didn't peek over her shoulder to check.

Half an hour later, she stood by the door. Every last thing of hers that had been here was in Michelle's car or her hands.

"Bye," Rory said. Michelle gave a small wave, which Helena returned, and then the two of them left as quietly as they'd come.

~~*

"I want you to come to a meeting with me," Rory said to Michelle.

"Am I allowed to be there?" Michelle asked.

"Yeah. Someone brought in their partner a couple of weeks ago." Rory held onto Michelle's hand. They were on their way to having dinner with Jason before the group. Rory had been chewing on the idea for most of the week. Now she'd come to a decision.

"All right," Michelle said, glancing at her indulgently from the driver's side of the car.

Jason was there before they arrived. He walked up to them with arms wide and a hug for each of them. Rory waited until after they'd ordered, and Michelle had ducked into the bathroom, before sharing her good news with Jason.

"Michelle told me she loves me." Rory couldn't contain it any longer. She was one of those giddy, totally in love girls, just so happy that the person she was in love with was in love with her too.

Jason's eyes opened wide. "When?" he asked, giving an over the top look around like he was making sure Michelle wasn't coming back just yet.

Rory laughed. "Just over a week ago. She also asked me to move in with her."

"I can't believe you didn't even text me! Rory... That's huge! Oh come on, come over here." He motioned her towards him, heedless of the table that was in the way, and grabbed her in for a hug.

"Oh no, hey hey," Michelle said, coming back. "I leave for two seconds and you've already got your hands all over my girl."

"Come here, you," Jason said with a mock growl, congratulating her with just as much effusion as he'd given to Rory. Michelle rolled her eyes, but she let him hug her, and even hugged him back. "Okay, this is a celebration. I'm buying you both dinner!"

"No—" Michelle started. Rory put her hand on Michelle's.

"We'd love you to," Rory said, looking between Michelle and Jason. "But only if you let us buy the next one."

"Done deal," Jason said, lifting his hand as the waiter came around.

The support group was a small one that week. Rory expected it to feel strange, walking in there with Michelle to support her. And it did. But it also felt important to have her there at least once, which was why she'd invited her to come.

She didn't speak up immediately. Nervousness held her tongue. She couldn't help but listen to the other peoples' stories around the room and try to imagine how Michelle was hearing it. She wasn't yet able to read Michelle's face like Michelle could read hers, not without her own insecurities getting in the way. But she was working on it.

"Hi, my name's Rory. Some of you already know me." She'd deliberately not held Michelle's hand in case Michelle didn't want the others in the room to link them, but Michelle reached out and took her hand as Rory started to speak. Jason, on the other side of her, began to smile. "I've been coming regularly for several months now. I've felt like I'm living on borrowed time until my next drink. Sometimes I still feel that way."

She looked towards Michelle, then back to the rest of the group again. She had no questions to ask this week, and only a few things she wanted to say.

"I've been sober more than a month now, which is the longest stretch I've managed since I started coming to these meetings, and it's been really hard. I can hide from uni most of the time, but classes are about to start again soon, and I'm a little bit worried about that. But I'm hoping I still have the strength, with my support network. And if I don't, then I'll just start the count again and do better next time."

She hoped her words were right. She wanted that. Now she just had to make it happen.

Fin

About the Author

Nicole writes across the spectrum of sexuality and gender identity. She lives in Melbourne with her fiancee, two cats, and a bottomless cup of tea. She likes candles, incense and Gilmore Girls.

Sign up for her newsletter and get a free copy of Rosellas in Flight. For this free story, go to: https://nicolefieldwrites.wordpress.com/2017/04/05/free-read-rosellas-in-flight/

She can be found on Goodreads: https://www.goodreads.com/author/show/6878229.Nicole_Field
Twitter: https://twitter.com/faerywhimsy
Tumblr: http://polynbooks.tumblr.com/

You might also enjoy…

EIGHT SECONDS

Sometimes you have to lose to win.

WILLIAM DAVRICK

ואהבת לרעך כמוך

NICE JEWISH BOYS

SARAH L. YOUNG

CONFLICT MANAGEMENT

RACHEL WHITE

A.F. HENLEY
WE THREE
KINGS

Made in the USA
Columbia, SC
01 April 2019